SERIES

Winter Hawk Star

Star

SIGMUND BROUWER

WORD PUBLISHING
Dallas • London • Vancouver • Melbourne

To Philip and Brandon—
Winter Hawks fans before they were born.

WINTER HAWK STAR

Copyright © 1996 by Sigmund Brouwer.

All rights reserved. No portion of this book may be
reproduced in any form without the written
permission of the publisher, except for
brief excerpts in reviews.

Managing Editor: Laura Minchew
Project Editor: Beverly Phillips

Library of Congress Cataloging–in–Publication Data

Brouwer, Sigmund, 1959–
    Winter hawk star / Sigmund Brouwer.
       p. cm.—(Lightning on ice series; 4)
    "Word kids!"
    Summary: Tyler Watson and his teammate, the star center for
the Portland Winter Hawks hockey team, discover that working
with street kids has placed their own lives in danger.
    ISBN 0–8499–3640–3
    [1. Hockey—Fiction. 2. Drug Abuse—Fiction. 3. Criminals—
Fiction.] I. Title. II. Series: Brouwer, Sigmund, 1959–
Lightning on ice series; 4.
PZ7.B79984Wl   1996
[Fic]—dc20

                            95–19516
                               CIP
                               AC

Printed in the United States of America
96 97 98 99 00 LBM 9 8 7 6 5 4 3 2 1

Winter Hawk Star

LIGHTNING ON ICE SERIES

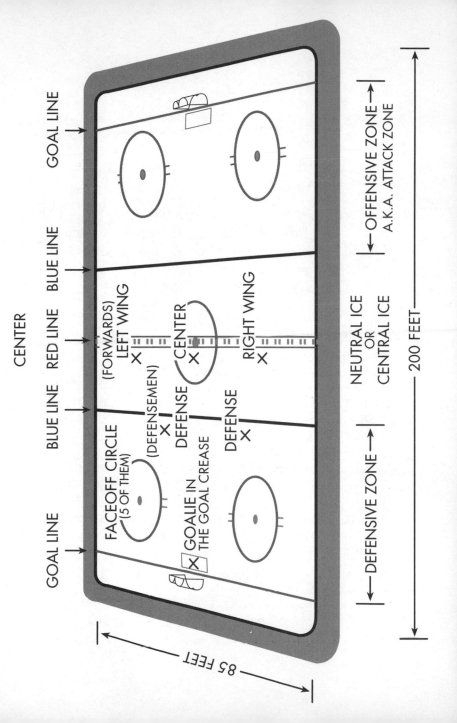

CENTER

GOAL LINE · BLUE LINE · RED LINE · BLUE LINE · BLUE LINE · GOAL LINE

(FORWARDS)
LEFT WING
X

CENTER
X

RIGHT WING
X

(DEFENSEMEN)
X
DEFENSE

DEFENSE
X

FACEOFF CIRCLE
(5 OF THEM)

X GOALIE IN
THE GOAL CREASE

|← DEFENSIVE ZONE →| |← NEUTRAL ICE
OR
CENTRAL ICE →| |← OFFENSIVE ZONE →|
A.K.A. ATTACK ZONE

|←——————— 200 FEET ———————→|

|←—— 85 FEET ——→|

Hockey Terms

For readers new to hockey, the following definitions may be helpful.

Assist: A player earns an assist by making a pass that is converted into a goal.

Blue line, red line, goal line: The length of the ice is roughly divided into thirds. One third up the ice from each end a blue line crosses the ice. The red line crosses the ice at the halfway point. At each of the far ends, a goal line crosses the ice (see diagram on page v).

Boards: The entire ice surface is enclosed by waist-high boards that are curved in the corners to match the oval of the rink. A Plexiglas shield above the boards protects the spectators from being hit by a stray puck.

Body check: In hockey, it is legal to run into the person with the puck as long as contact is made with the upper body or hips.

Breakaway: A breakaway occurs when a player with the puck has no one between him and the opposing goalie.

Faceoff: A faceoff occurs at the beginning of each period and after each stoppage of play. The referee drops the puck in a faceoff circle to start play, and the center from each team tries to gain control of the puck.

Forechecker: When a forward or forwards are sent deep into the offensive zone after the puck or puck carrier, they are called forecheckers.

Hat trick: Any time a player scores three goals in one game, it is called a "hat trick."

Hipcheck: A hipcheck is similar to a body check except contact is made as the hip is swung outward.

Icing: An icing penalty is called when a player shoots from behind his blue line and the puck travels all the way across the goal line at the far end. It results in a faceoff in the penalized player's end zone, which cancels the advantage of having moved the puck so far.

Neutral zone trap: This is a strategy of sending one man in to forecheck, leaving four skaters in the center ice area.

One-time: The process of hitting the puck without first stopping it.

Overtime: Overtime rules vary in different leagues. In the WHL, it consists of ten minutes of extra play. The first team to score in the extra time wins the game (called sudden-death overtime). In regular season play, a tie at the end of overtime remains a tie. In playoff games, overtime is played until a goal is scored to break the tie.

Period: A regular hockey game consists of sixty minutes of play, divided into three twenty-minute periods.

Point: (1) A single point is given for a goal. (2) In team standings, zero points are accumulated for a loss, one point for a tie, and two points for a win. (3) When a defenseman is standing inside the opposition's blue line, his position is also referred to as "standing at the point."

Power play: Penalties in hockey result in the offending player "serving time" in the penalty box. This time varies according to the penalty. With one and sometimes two fewer players on the ice, the penalized team is at a tremendous disadvantage. The unpenalized team is then considered to be on the power play. It is also known as a "man advantage" or a "two-man advantage."

Slap shot: A slap shot is the hardest shot in hockey. A player raises his stick above his shoulders before swinging downward to "slap" the shot. Slap shots have been recorded at speeds of well over 100 miles per hour.

Stickhandle: To control the puck by moving it from side to side with the blade of the hockey stick.

Two-on-one, three-on-one, four-on-one, and so on: If there is only one defenseman between the goalie and two attackers with the puck, it is called a "two-on-one"; the other numbers correspond to the various situations.

Zone: The ice surface is broken into three zones. The areas behind each of the two blue lines are known as the end zones; the central area between both blue lines is the neutral zone.

One

When I think of the hockey play that made Riley Judd an instant rookie legend, I always remember it beginning where he's alone against two Spokane Chiefs defensemen.

After all, most times a forward should not be able to beat even one defenseman. The defensemen have too many options. They can knock the puck away, body check* the forward, block the shot, or move the forward to the side.

Not only was Riley facing two of them alone, but our team was also trying to kill off a penalty. It was late in the game, tied at six goals each. The screaming hometown crowd was going wild. A goal for us would be a huge break. But next to impossible.

And Riley was at center ice, puck on his stick, trying the impossible against those two Chiefs defensemen.

"Come on, rookie!" It was Brett Beckham yelling, the

---

* An asterisk in the text indicates a hockey term that is in the list of definitions on pages vi–viii.

1

left defenseman, veteran all-star for the Chiefs. The same Brett Beckham that Riley had made look like a fool on an earlier breakaway*. "We're gonna eat your lunch!"

Riley put his head down and pushed the puck up the ice, angling for the opening between the two defensemen. Beckham swung toward his partner, going for a body check that would knock Riley into next week.

At the last second, Riley flipped the puck between them and did a little duck-and-shuffle so complicated I wasn't sure if I had seen it right. It pretzeled one of the defensemen and left Beckham jumping at open air.

Riley squirted through, calmly picked up the puck, and closed the gap between him and the goalie.

Beckham turned and chased Riley, bawling out angry words. "Never again, rookie! Never again!"

Riley paused. It was hardly more than a half-step pause, as if he were considering Beckham's words.

Then Riley put his head down again and broke across the final bit of open ice toward the goalie. Riley pulled the puck into his skates, pretended he was going to push it out again, and yanked it to his backhand instead. The goalie fell for it, sprawling across the left side of the net.

That left Riley the entire right side of the net, with the puck on his backhand, only inches away from the wide-open goal line.

I couldn't believe it. Riley didn't flip the puck into

the net to put us ahead. He actually held on to the puck and continued around the Chiefs' net.

It stunned the crowd into silence. Riley Judd had just given up a chance at his third goal of the game.

He came out from behind the other side of the net—still with the puck—and skated back toward our goalie.

It was crazy, unexpected. Everybody, I'm sure, was asking the same question that was going through my head: *What was Riley Judd doing?*

I'd seen a lot from the players' bench before, but nothing like this. Of course, as a fourth-line winger, I see a lot from the bench. A lot of goals. A lot of penalties. A lot of line changes as players step onto the ice. Unfortunately, too few of those line changes include me. What I see most are the backs of the helmets of the guys who get to play while I stay behind on the bench.

Tonight, Riley Judd, playing the center ice position, was one of those guys who stepped past me onto the ice again and again. Only sixteen years old, this was his first game with the Portland Winter Hawks. In fact, it was his first game in the Western Hockey League. I knew it. The fans knew it. The media knew it. Everyone knew it. Half the reason the stands were so full was because of Riley Judd, Superstar.

He hadn't disappointed anyone either, not with two goals and an assist* already. Judd's two goals had been real beauties, forcing me to agree with the newspaper articles that labeled him a superstar. He'd definitely shown the crowd he was Portland's new star. All it took was for him to get the puck, and our hometown crowd instantly raised their already deafening volume of yelling and cheering.

Except for now. The silence in the stands was the kind of silence that happens just after a car accident.

What was Riley Judd doing?

He busted hard toward *our* net, meeting the same two defensemen he had just beaten twenty seconds earlier on his way to *their* net. Beckham took a swipe at the puck, but Riley skated a wide circle, leaving Beckham to stand and stare in the same disbelief shared by everyone in the rink.

Riley reached their blue line* on his way out of their end toward ours. He didn't stop. Two Chiefs' forwards moved in on him. Riley faked a move left, sprinted to the right, and reached open ice near the center line.

Now Riley was skating in on our defensemen, as if he were a Chiefs' forward. Two of the Chiefs were chasing him. Everyone else on the ice was moving slowly, staring at Riley, trying to understand.

As he moved toward our blue line and closer to our net, I saw stunned expressions on the faces of each of our defensemen. *Were they supposed to try to check their own teammate?*

Riley spared them the need to decide. When he reached our blue line, he spun a tight circle, keeping the puck on his stick as if it had been taped to the blade.

At that moment, I understood.

He was going to take another run at their net. Only now, there were five Chiefs' skaters between him and their goalie, not just the two defensemen.

Seconds later, as he started up the ice again, the crowd understood the same thing I did.

Their cheers returned in a screaming frenzy.

Riley slowed almost to a stop. He dipsy-doodled in small circles as one forward tried to hit him, then another. With each step Riley took, he kept the puck, dangling it like a yo-yo just out of a baby's reach.

If I had been one of the Chiefs on the ice, I would have gone crazy too. They forgot about playing smart positional hockey and moved in on him, wolves pouncing for hamburger.

Riley scooted through the center ice area and came out near their blue line.

Again, it was just him against two defenseman.

"Never again?" Riley asked in a clear yell. "How's now?"

Beckham was so mad he dropped his stick and tried to tackle Riley.

Riley stopped, ducked, and let Beckham rush past him. Beckham tumbled into the other defenseman. As they tried to untangle themselves, Riley carried the puck toward the goalie—his second breakaway of the same shift on the ice.

Against all logic, Riley made the exact same move he had made on the first breakaway. He was so smooth, so good, the goalie had no choice but to fall the same way, backward into the left side of the net.

Riley stopped, backed up, turned his head to watch Beckham charge, then finally slapped the puck into the open net. The crowd erupted into a roar so loud it would have been impossible to hear a jet take off.

Everyone in the rink gave him a standing ovation.

And when he skated back to the bench, Coach Estleman suspended him for two games. Riley watched the rest of the game sitting beside me.

Two

As a fourth-line winger, I'm nearly invisible. Sure, Coach Estleman knows my name. It's Tyler Watson. He understands my style of play. He knows what to expect from me on the ice. Other than that, I tend to fade into the background for him. There are twenty other players who get more of his time because those twenty better players have bigger roles in making our team win.

I'm not complaining though. It's a thrill for me just to be on the Portland Winter Hawks. I mean, someone has to fill in on the fourth line, and it might as well be me. The other guys can dream about making it from here in the Western Hockey League to the National Hockey League. I don't. I just want to be able to put in my shifts without making any mistakes.

I suppose I could be less invisible to Coach Estleman if I were one of the guys who joked around in the locker room. Or if I broke curfew. Or if I complained. It's just easier to not be noticed. That way people don't expect things from you. There's no pressure, nothing to fear.

In fact, when Scotty, our team trainer, stopped in the dressing room after practice and told me that Coach Estleman wanted to see me in his office, I began to worry right away.

What could I have done wrong? I'd skated hard in practice. During last night's game against the Chiefs, I'd only been on the ice a dozen times. Not enough time to make many mistakes. For that matter, no one had scored on us during any of my shifts. And we won 7–6, thanks to Riley Judd's last goal.

I got out of my hockey equipment quickly, showered as fast as possible and dressed in a hurry. I didn't want to keep Coach Estleman waiting.

I left behind the steamy dressing room and the shouting and joke telling of the guys relaxing after practice. I half jogged to Coach Estleman's office.

He stood when I knocked on his door. He walked over and greeted me with a handshake. This was not good. He never shook my hand. *Was he going to give me bad news? Was he going to tell me they had decided to let me go from the team?*

"Tyler," he said, "I've got a favor to ask."

I braced myself. Maybe he was going to ask me to understand his point of view. Maybe he wanted me to make it easy on him as he let me go from the team.

"Sure, Coach," I said. "Anything you need."

He looked me straight in the eyes, which meant he was six feet tall, just like me. Of course, we were different in plenty of other ways. He was forty-something. I was eighteen. He had blond hair combed sideways over the top of his head to try to hide the fact that he was going bald. I had red hair, cut short because I hate combing it at all. He wore a gray suit. I wore jeans, a T-shirt, leather jacket, and cowboy boots.

"Why don't you sit down," he said, pointing to a chair in the corner of the office.

Although we did host a few games in the new Rose Garden where the Portland Trailblazers play NBA basketball, we mostly played and practiced in the Memorial Coliseum, where Coach Estleman kept his office. It had thick new carpet, wood paneling on the walls, and some art pieces with weird shapes that I couldn't understand.

I moved across the thick carpet and sat in the chair. He was seated behind his desk.

I didn't know where to put my hands. I didn't know where to look. I didn't want to look directly at him and make him think I was being disrespectful. I didn't want to keep staring around at everything in his office and make him think I was rude.

"Tyler," he began, "you study the game. You understand the plays. You work hard."

All of it was true. I hoped, though, he wouldn't add the other stuff about my game. Like I couldn't skate quite as fast as the guys on the first, second, and third lines. That too many of my shots floated toward the goalie like plump marshmallows. Or that when I had the puck I got flustered and never seemed to make a

9

great pass. To me, it seemed like time sped up on the ice, and I never knew quite what to do as the play unfolded around me.

He frowned. "It's like you have all the tools, but you just don't want to use them."

"Sir?"

"I'll tell you the straight goods," he said.

I felt my stomach go into a knot. This was beginning to sound like a bad-news situation.

"Yes?"

"You know the situation in this league with most eighteen-year-olds."

I did. Sixteen- and seventeen-year-olds—unless they were superstars like Riley—spent their first years in the league developing their skills. At eighteen, they were expected to be team leaders and good, solid players.

"Since day one, Tyler, it's been obvious to this organization that you have potential. In your first year, we thought things didn't go well because you were a rookie. Last year, we told ourselves that any game you would start to prove yourself. That game never arrived. We've been waiting and waiting for you to do some-thing, but it seems you're happy to just fill a uniform."

Where was this going?

"Well, I—"

"We can't afford to keep an eighteen-year-old who doesn't perform." He shook his head sadly. "Tyler, we've even put out feelers to see if anyone will take you in a trade. No one has been interested. They've all said the same thing. Tyler Watson doesn't contribute."

"Well, I—"

"We're not going to cut you, Tyler. Not yet."

Was this good news or bad?

"You've got another month. Maybe six weeks. If you don't start playing like you want to play, we're going to have to let you go."

"I'll do my best," I said. I began to stand.

"Not so fast," Coach Estleman said. "There's a string attached. I'm going to ask a favor. It's about Riley Judd."

Coach shook his head. "Here's a kid with as much talent, maybe more talent, than Wayne Gretzky. But he's heard that ever since he was six years old. Unlike Gretzky, Judd believes he should be treated like a star."

Now I really wondered where this was going.

"Riley Judd is the best player this league has seen in twenty years. I'll never coach someone this good again. Almost by himself, Judd can take our team to the championship finals. Even with his bad attitude."

Coach managed to grin. "Hey, how many coaches would kill to have this kind of problem?"

I squinted. The question mark must have been all over my face.

"Yes," he said, "a problem. Hockey's a team game. It involves discipline. That stunt he pulled last night is unforgivable. What if this had been a playoff game? What if he hadn't scored? He might be the best player in the world, but I can't let him get away with what he did. It will hurt the team. And, in the long run, it will hurt him. When he hits the NHL, he's got to have more than just talent."

11

Coach Estleman paused and tapped his desk with a pencil. "Tyler, you're a lot smarter than you think you are. So tell me, what's my problem?"

"Judd's a million-dollar player. You're not a million-dollar coach."

"Obviously you read the sports section of the newspaper today."

"Yes, sir."

"And you heard the fans scream for my blood last night when I refused to let him play for the rest of the game. Unhappy fans means an unhappy team owner."

"Yes, sir."

"What this creates is a power struggle. Riley against me," Coach said. "Unfortunately, if it comes down to it, I think the owner would get rid of me before getting rid of Judd."

I nodded. Riley Judd *was* that good.

"Even if I could trade him away," Coach said, "I wouldn't want to. The kid is a joy to watch."

I really, really wondered where this was going and why I was in the coach's office hearing this.

"Fortunately, the owner does agree with me on one thing. If Riley Judd doesn't make an attitude adjustment, it will hurt the team. And it will hurt Riley Judd. He's got to learn the world doesn't revolve around him just because he's a star hockey player."

"Coach?"

"This year, the public relations people have gotten us involved with a group called Youth Works. It's an inner-city organization that helps kids from disadvantaged backgrounds." Coach Estleman shrugged. "The owner knows someone on the board of directors of Youth Works. One night they had dinner together and came up with the idea to send a couple of players from the team to help the kids."

Coach Estleman pointed at me. "You're one of the players. Riley will be the other. Maybe that way Riley will learn something about real life. You're both going into the inner city to do some volunteer work on behalf of the Winter Hawks."

"Me, sir?" This didn't sound like I was volunteering.

"Look, Tyler. You're a sensible kid. That's why I'm explaining all this to you. Which, by the way, you're not going to repeat to Riley Judd. Right?"

"Right, sir."

"Your job is to make sure he actually spends time with the kids. We'll even give you gas money for driving him there and back. Your job is to make sure he doesn't get in trouble. Your job is to be a good influence on Riley Judd."

"Yes, sir."

"You'll spend four hours a week at the organization. Every Tuesday and Thursday afternoon, you and Riley will represent the Winter Hawks and spend time with the kids, doing whatever the people there see fit."

"But, I—"

"Do you want six weeks to prove yourself? It's either go to Youth Works or get cut from the team. That's the same choice I offered Riley. With Riley, though he doesn't know it, I was bluffing. With you, I'm not."

He stared at me, waiting for my answer.

"What time did you want us there, Coach?" I asked. "And what's the address?"

Three

I don't have to do this," Riley Judd told me.

I was looking for street signs as I drove, so I ignored him. Besides, he'd been saying that since he got in my Jeep Cherokee a half hour earlier. He was saying it just to get me to argue with him. The truth was, as far as he knew, he *did* have to do this. Part of the contract that we sign as WHL players states that we will make ourselves available for public functions as Winter Hawks players.

"Third Avenue," I said. "We're getting closer. Coach told us to look for the gate."

"Gate? That sounds dumb. All of this sounds dumb."

"The Chinatown gate. Cross the Willamette River on Burnside Bridge. Around Fourth Avenue look for," I pointed, "the Chinatown gate. See?"

Riley quit grumbling long enough to look.

The huge gate had three different levels, all brightly painted in complicated patterns. On each side were huge bronze lions.

"Cool," Riley said, although by the tone of his voice he meant otherwise. "First, you're a taxi driver. Now a tour guide?"

I nearly told him I felt like a baby-sitter, but I managed to keep my mouth shut.

It was four o'clock, so afternoon traffic was heavy. We sat through the stoplight twice before reaching Fifth Avenue where I turned right. We drove another few minutes. It didn't take long before the buildings we were passing began to look run down. There were vacant lots. Instead of clothing shops and cafes and people on the sidewalks enjoying September sunshine, there were old houses, old apartments, and two-story factory buildings.

We passed a man in a big brown overcoat. He was pushing a shopping cart filled with empty bottles.

"Nice neighborhood," Riley said, again not meaning what he said.

"The kids we're visiting have to grow up in this area."

"They should have been smart enough to be born into different families."

What a jerk. I slammed on the brakes. It snapped Riley ahead into his seat belt.

"Hey! Why'd you do that?"

"We're here," I said. "Youth Works."

Just as Coach Estleman had promised, the building had been easy to find. All I had to do was keep my eyes open for the steeple and large cross. Youth Works had bought a large brick church building, built years and years earlier when wealthy people had lived in the area. The church building was set back from the street. I was willing to bet it was at least a hundred years old.

In fading letters on a dirty white background, the sign stuck crookedly into the ground read: HOME TO YOUTH WORKS.

The lawn between the sidewalk and the church was worn down, almost lumpy. I could guess why. A swing set and slide took most of the middle of it. About twenty kids took the rest of it. They were running and screaming and doing all the things kids do when you let them loose outside.

"We might as well get started," I said. "We're supposed to ask for someone named Sam."

"Probably some dry, dusty old janitor type," Riley said. "I think I'll wait in the car."

"Suit yourself."

"I always do," Riley said. "In fact, I think I'll just wait in the car for the entire two hours. Tell me what it was like when you get back."

"Suit yourself."

I left him there and crossed the hard ground of the lawn. The kids ignored me. They had more important things on their minds. Like yelling and screaming and chasing each other.

I managed to make it across without stepping on any of them. I knocked on a set of doors at the side of the church building. Within thirty seconds, the door swung open.

I found it hard to speak. I almost found it hard to

breathe. A girl who looks like she just stepped out of a magazine ad will do that to a guy.

She wore blue jeans and a white T-shirt. She had long dark hair that hung in loose curls. She had deep brown eyes. She had a slow, wide smile. She had me in the palm of her hand.

"Hello?" she said. It might have been her second or third hello. I was still trying to find air to speak.

"Um," I said.

She laughed. "That's a good start. Are you from the Portland Winter Hawks?"

"Um," I said.

"I can guess by your jacket."

I looked down. Of course. My team jacket. The one with Portland Winter Hawks all over it.

"Um," I said.

"We've been expecting you," she said. Her smile became a slight frown. "But I thought there would be two of you."

"Um," I said.

"Oh, there he is." She looked past me, at my car. I looked with her. Riley was jogging across the grass toward us with a big grin on his face. He neatly side-stepped a couple of kids, as if he were a football player on his way to a touchdown.

"Um," I said.

Riley slapped me on the back as he joined us.

"Hey, bud," he said. "Next time wait for me to get my shoes tied, will you?"

He turned his grin toward the girl in the doorway.

Riley is nearly my height. He has dark hair and blue eyes and a dimple in the center of his chin. He fills his Portland Winter Hawks jacket like he's lifted weights since he was ten years old, which, of course, he has. He has an Elvis strut that shows he's afraid of no one. With my short red hair and too many freckles on a face with no dimples and no wonderful smile, I was just a mutt wagging his tail beside a show dog.

"The name's Riley Judd," he said to the girl. He stuck his hand out for her to shake, which she did. With a nice big smile for him.

"I've been looking forward to helping out with the kids. In a neighborhood like this, they need as many breaks as they can get." Riley shook his head sadly in sympathy for them. "The big guy here hasn't been so keen, but we'll work on him, right?"

She laughed. Riley was still holding her hand. "Right," she said. "We'll work on him."

The screams of laughter on the lawn rose and fell as they continued to hold hands and look at each other.

Riley finally let go of her hand. "Well," he said, "the first thing we need to do is talk to someone named Sam. Any chance you can help us?"

"I'm Sam," she said. "I'm in charge of the phys-ed programs here."

"You're Sam?" Riley asked. "You don't look like a Sam."

"Um," I said.

"Actually, I'm Samantha. Samantha Blair."

"Sam for short," Riley said. "I like that. It's kind of classy."

She rewarded him with another smile.

"You don't look much older than us," Riley said.

"I'm eighteen. I skipped a grade in elementary school. Graduated high school early. I'm taking a year off to work with the kids before I go to college."

"Um," I said. *Why could Riley find things to say, and why did my tongue feel like a block of wood?*

"It's great that you guys could help," she said. "Mostly, we just want you to spend time with the kids. A lot of them come from broken homes. Youth Works is a place where they don't have to worry about getting beat up by parents or gang members. When school finishes for the day, they come here instead of going home. We try to make sure they get exercise, good food, and a friendly ear to listen to their problems. We—"

She stopped herself and shot a startled glance over our shoulders.

"That's my brother, Ben! What are they doing with him?"

We followed her gaze. Two men were standing in the middle of a bunch of kids. They had grabbed a seven- or eight-year-old kid by his arms and were dragging him toward the open side door of a blue van parked in front of my Jeep.

From the ski masks over their faces, it was easy to guess they weren't Ben's friends.

Four

They threw Ben into the van. One of the men jumped in behind him and slid the door shut. The other man ran around the front of the van and jumped behind the steering wheel.

"You drove, right?" Samantha asked.

I nodded. The keys to my Jeep were still dangling in my hand.

She grabbed my wrist and started dragging me toward the street. I stumbled after her. The kids on the lawn were all frozen in shock, quiet and staring in the direction of the disappearing van.

"What about me?" Riley shouted.

"Call the police!" she shouted over her shoulder. "Tell them what happened!"

I had to run to keep up with her. The kids made room for us as we passed through the group.

I sprinted past her, cutting around the front of the Jeep and sliding in behind the steering wheel as she managed to get in the passenger side.

The Jeep started with a roar. I gunned it, and we jumped ahead.

"Seat belt!" I shouted. I scrambled to get mine on before we squealed around the first corner.

The van was a block away.

I pressed the gas pedal to the floor. We closed the gap to half a block.

"License plates," I told her. Time seemed to be like a slow current. I felt strangely calm and clearheaded. "Get the number. There's pen and paper in the glove box."

She scrambled to find the paper. I concentrated on the road.

Now the van was a quarter block away. Close enough to see the plates. Close enough to see we wouldn't get the number.

Samantha slammed the dash with her fist in frustration. The back end of the blue van was covered with mud, and the van's license plates were impossible to see.

At that moment, the van driver must have realized we were chasing him. A huge cloud of black smoke mushroomed from the van's exhaust pipe, and it started to slip away.

I glanced at my speedometer. *Fifty miles an hour.* I thought of the rush-hour traffic on the main roads. He'd be forced to slow down as soon as we got off these side streets.

Brake lights suddenly showed on the van. It skidded sideways to make a right turn at the next intersection.

I slammed on my own brakes and wrestled with the steering wheel to keep from sliding out of control. I turned hard to make the corner.

The van had turned maybe five seconds before we reached the intersection. And five seconds earlier, both lanes had been clear. The van had been able to skid through the far lane, then veer back onto the right side of the road.

Not us. In those five seconds, a small truck had almost reached the stop sign of the cross street. And we were also skidding into the far lane, a half second away from slamming into it head-on.

I made a decision without even thinking. Instead of fighting the skid and trying to pull back into our lane, I spun the wheel to the left, aiming for the sidewalk on the other side of the truck.

For one sickening heartbeat, I thought we were dead. I braced, ready for the crash. And in the next second, we hit the edge of the sidewalk, hard enough for our seat belts to jerk us back on to the seats.

I kept my grip on the steering wheel, holding tight, trying to keep us on a straight line down the sidewalk.

Fire hydrant.

I spun the wheel again, cranking us back on to the street, missing the fire hydrant by less than the thickness of a coat of paint. We bounced off the side-walk, shot through a gap of parked cars, and hit open pavement.

The van had opened its lead to a full block again.

I mashed the gas pedal and tried to catch up.

The van's brake lights showed red again. It made another turn to the right.

This time, I was ready for the corner. I eased off the gas, hitting the brakes hard. We rounded this corner under control.

I stomped the gas yet again, throwing us back against the bucket seats of the Jeep. In the next split second, I almost stood on the brakes.

We had rounded the corner to see a huge delivery truck angled across the street, backing into an alley. The delivery truck seemed to fill our entire windshield.

Five

I managed to stop a dozen steps from the side of the delivery truck. The blue van had not. It was resting sideways against the truck. The driver must have skidded sideways trying to stop and turn away from it. The van now blocked the delivery truck driver's door. The driver stared down at the top of the van from behind his own steering wheel.

"My brother!" Samantha shouted.

She yanked at the door handle and popped the door open. In her panic, she forgot the seat belt. It caught in her hair.

"Don't get out," I said.

"But my brother! He's in the van."

"The guys who kidnapped him are also in the—"

I snapped my mouth shut. The sliding door on the van was opening, and they were getting out of the van. Two of them, not wearing ski masks now. The taller one had a walrus mustache. The shorter one had blond hair that reached his shoulders.

The one with the walrus mustache reached back with his free hand and dragged Ben from the van.

Without taking my eyes off them, I reached into the backseat. I knew exactly what I was going to grab. One of my hockey sticks on top of my gym bag.

I closed my hand on the shaft of wood and pulled the stick with me as I stepped out of the Jeep.

"Leave the kid," I said.

"Drop dead," the short, blond-haired guy said.

"Leave him." I wasn't going to let them take the kid.

"Drop dead," he repeated. "We'll give you the help you need to do it."

His partner pulled out a switchblade knife. He clicked it open.

Again, I felt a strange calmness. I gripped the stick like a baseball bat. I measured the distance between us. Instead of backing up, I took a step closer.

"Come on, boys," I said. "Try me out."

The second one pulled out a switchblade.

I grinned. A part of me wondered where my fearlessness was coming from. Another part of me got ready to swing hard and swing smart.

They split up. One moved to my left. One moved to my right. I couldn't defend myself against them both.

But the boy was free.

"Run hard, kid!" I shouted. "Take the chance now."

The boy sprinted toward me. Then passed me.

"You're meat," the guy with the mustache snarled, waving his knife. "Sliced, bloody meat."

"And you're a home run," I said, gripping my stick harder.

The sound of sirens reached us.

The men looked at each other and hesitated.

In that moment, I stepped forward and swung hard at the one on the right. He managed to get his arm up. I broke my stick across his forearm.

He shrieked.

Sirens rose louder.

The other one moved in close, stabbing at air.

I was left with half a hockey stick in my hands. I swung it at him, and he danced away.

His partner kept shrieking in agony.

I heard the Jeep's door slam shut.

"I'm with you!" Sam shouted.

"And me," a strange voice said. It belonged to the driver of the delivery truck, rounding the back of his vehicle. He carried a tire iron in his hand.

Both kidnappers reacted instantly. They ran across the street and into the alley.

I stared after them, suddenly aware that I was breathing hard and fast.

Time returned to normal speed. I began to realize what I had just done—I'd held my own against two men armed with switchblades.

"Leave them be," Sam said. "We got my brother back. We don't need to chase them."

I managed to nod. *Like I was stupid enough to run after them?*

"Sorry, kid," the truck driver growled. "It took me

awhile to get out the passenger side of my truck. I had some boxes in the front seat."

He was a big man. Dirty blue jeans. Dirty black shirt. Big beer belly. I was glad he'd been on my side.

I managed to nod to him too. *Had all of this really happened?*

Sam's brother joined us. A kid with brown hair, his head hardly reached as high as her shoulders. He stood beside his sister, his arms wrapped around her waist. I found out later that Ben was allowed to participate in Youth Works activities because his sister worked there.

"You don't speak much, do you?" Sam said to me.

"Um," I said. Something about her grin and the way her hair blew across her face tangled my heart and my tongue.

"What's your name anyway?" she asked.

"Um," I said again.

Where was my sense of calm when I really needed it?

Six

"H_{ey}, hero," Riley Judd told me, "prepare to look stupid."

We stood almost visor to visor at the center line during practice.

"Hero?" I asked. He stood on one side of the center line. I stood on the other.

"You didn't see me chasing down a van, did you? You didn't see me getting thank-you hugs from Sam."

I still couldn't believe I'd actually faced down two guys with switchblades the day before. I didn't expect anyone on the team to believe it either. They'd probably laugh at me. I preferred to be invisible. A person stayed out of trouble that way.

"How many times do I have to tell you it wasn't a big deal," I said. "Sam was probably just happy to get her brother back and—"

The piercing blast of Coach Estleman's whistle interrupted me.

"You clowns going to gab all afternoon?" Coach asked as he skated toward us. "Or are you ready to play?"

"Ready to play," I said. "Sorry, Coach."

"Play?" Riley Judd said. He pushed his helmet back to look me directly in the face. "Play? I'm ready to put on a show."

I sure hoped he wouldn't. For the first half hour, we had skated hard during this practice. We had then spent twenty minutes in shooting drills, another twenty minutes in passing drills. Now we would finish with a half hour of scrimmage. Reds against blues—half the team against the other half in a game situation.

During the entire scrimmage, our fourth line would play against the first line. When we rested, the second and third lines would play each other. We would continue to alternate until the end of the scrimmage.

I wore a red jersey. Riley Judd wore the blue. If Riley did put on a show, it would be directly against us reds. Worse, Riley was my man to guard. If he played great, the person looking like a fool would be me.

It didn't take him long to embarrass me.

The puck went into their end. Riley took a pass from the defenseman, and skated directly toward me with the puck.

I must have been frowning with concentration, because he glanced at my face and laughed.

"Not a chance," he said. "Watch this."

He faked a pass to his center. I didn't go for the fake. It would have been better if I had.

Instead of trying to slide the puck past me, Riley

snapped a quick hard wrist shot into the middle of my belly.

"Oof," I said, clutching myself as the puck dropped between my skates.

Riley snaked his stick ahead of him, pushed the puck all the way through my skates, cut around me, and cruised down the boards*. His laughter echoed throughout the empty arena.

His wasn't the only laughter, though. The rest of the guys found it funny too.

I wish that had been the only time he made me look dumb.

But no, it seemed every time he touched the puck, he showed me another unbelievable move to sucker me.

In a way, though, I had to admire him. At ice level, playing against him, I was able to understand what made him a superstar, although just by looking at him, you wouldn't think he was one of the greats. He wasn't as big as most of the players. He wasn't as fast. He didn't have an overpowering shot.

Instead, he seemed to have a sixth sense that told him where everybody was on the ice. It was like all ten skaters were players on a chess board, and he knew every move each of them would make and where the puck would go.

To go along with his uncanny ability to read each developing play, he could handle the puck as if it were nailed to the end of his hockey stick. He didn't need to be big or fast or overpowering. He slipped and slid through crowds of players as if he were oil poured through marbles, and when he reached open ice on the other side of the crowd, the puck would still be on his stick.

It was actually fun to watch him. Although it would have been nice to have him on my line instead of against me.

No matter what I did, he got past me. In fact, he scored ten goals during the scrimmage.

I don't usually get frustrated. Trouble was, every time he beat me, he laughed.

With two minutes left in the scrimmage, it was the same old situation. Puck behind their net. Defenseman passed the puck to Riley. I had to go chase him.

This time, Riley went to my right. He stopped, spun around backward, flipped the puck between his legs in the opposite direction, jumped over my stick and found open ice again.

I screamed in frustration.

Again, laughter.

I put my head down and chased him hard.

At their blue line, I almost caught him. Until he put on a little burst of speed and slipped away. At the center line, I almost caught him again. He danced just out of reach. At our blue line, he slowed and I nearly reached him.

He laughed again. I realized he was slowing down just to give me a chance.

I screamed again. No way was he going to score goal number eleven.

But he did. He cut to the inside and lifted his stick

to let the puck stop. He kicked it ahead with a skate back onto his stick. Then he fired a low hard screamer into the left side of the net, using the defenseman to screen the goalie.

I screamed yet again.

The goalie dug the puck out of the net and flipped it toward me.

I was so mad that as the puck reached me, I half turned, dropped my head and blasted a slap shot* away from all the players into the corner boards.

Only just as the puck was leaving my stick and just as I was lifting my head to see where the puck was going, I noticed trouble. Big trouble.

Coach Estleman, thinking he was well out of the way of the scrimmage, had drifted into the corner. His hands were in his pockets. Right where my hundred-mile-an-hour slap shot was about to hit.

For that split second, we stared at each other. I wondered if my face had the same expression of horror that his face did. Because we both knew the puck was headed for an area a few inches below his belt buckle.

Coach Estleman made a big mistake. He should have tried to block the puck by pulling his hands out of his pockets. Instead, he jumped up, hoping the puck would go between his legs.

It didn't.

The puck drilled him solid. Right where his legs joined together.

His face showed instant disbelief. The kind of disbelief that comes when you know that you've been hit there, but you don't feel the pain yet because it is still traveling up your body. But you know how bad it's going to be and any second the pain's going to reach your brain.

It reached his brain. His face puckered as he tried to get air. He doubled over, sagging to the ice like a deflating beach ball.

Coach Estleman curled up on the ice and moaned in agony.

Riley skated up to me and tapped me on the shoulder.

"Nice shot, Watson," he said. "But shooting drills ended a half hour ago."

It took Coach Estleman fifteen minutes to get to his feet again. The first thing he did was suspend me for three games.

So much for trying to stay invisible and out of trouble.

 **Seven**

On Tuesday, two of my suspended games later, Riley and I made another visit to Youth Works.

During the two games I watched from the stands, Riley had managed to collect five goals, four assists, and what seemed like a file a couple of inches thick of newspaper clippings.

Me? I had managed to collect a cold from a lady who sneezed on me in the first game, and popcorn in my hair from a kid who had spilled his bucket during the second game.

I thought about this as I parked the Jeep near the old brick church building. I was not in a good mood to be baby-sitting Riley Judd through another visit to Youth Works.

I was in a worse mood after an hour and a half with the little monsters of our assigned group.

"Are they always like this?" I asked Samantha. She had just walked into the room to check on our group.

Youth Works was big enough that she supervised volunteers working with kids in five different age groups. Today, Riley and I were stuck with just the eight- and nine-year-olds.

Although my stomach still danced with nervousness around her, I was finally able to speak to her without my teeth getting in the way of my tongue. It must have helped that I remembered how she had spent ten minutes hugging me for helping to save her brother from the guys with switchblades.

Samantha surveyed the room with me. It was the size of a regular classroom, tucked in a back hall of the church building. It had old couches, posters of rock stars on the wall, and fifteen kids jumping, screaming, and spitting paper wads at each other.

"You can speak!" she said with mock surprise.

"Last week I had, um, a dentist appointment," I said. I decided the floor would be interesting to stare at. Maybe I really could speak to her, but I couldn't quite look her right in those beautiful eyes. "My mouth was frozen when we got here. That's why I didn't say much. Really."

She grinned, like she knew that I knew that she knew that I was making it up.

"Anyway," she said, "these kids are on good behavior today. They think it's cool you guys are hockey players."

"Well," I said, "at least one of us is."

"What?" she asked.

"Nothing." Hockey was a depressing subject to me. So I changed it. "Your brother okay after last week?"

She nodded. A pillow flew over our heads.

"Any idea why those guys took him?" I hadn't had a chance to talk to her. After the police had shown up—interrupting the hug that I was enjoying so much—we had become too busy answering their questions to speak to each other.

"No idea," she said. She raised her voice to a couple of grimy-faced kids. "Johnny, take your hands off Bobby's neck!"

Johnny grinned. Bobby grinned. Johnny let go of Bobby's neck. Bobby promptly grabbed Johnny's neck.

"These kids are something," she said. "This group is full of kids who have real trouble in school."

She shook her head in sympathy for them. "But they really don't have a chance. Their parents hit them or yell at them all the time. Some don't get a decent meal for days. Others are even left alone for days, while their parents wander the bars. And a lot of them have serious medical problems. How can they really fit into an organized classroom?"

"Yeah," I said, not sure if I meant it. To me, they looked like brats. Three of them had jumped on Riley, and he was staggering around with them hanging from his waist and shoulders.

"No idea why those guys kidnapped your brother?" I repeated. "How about the van? Did you find out who it belonged to?"

"Joey!" she yelled. "I know it's a Nerf bat, but it can still hurt."

The kid grinned and kept whacking another boy over the head with the soft foam bat.

"The police told me it belonged to some pharmaceutical company," she answered as if we hadn't been interrupted.

"Pharmaceutical companies are into kidnapping?"

She laughed. "No, silly. The van had been stolen from the company."

"Oh."

Her face suddenly showed alarm, and she looked around the room wildly. "Ben! Where's Ben!"

Her little brother was not among the kids jumping around this room.

I put my fingers in my mouth and whistled. Loud.

It froze most of the kids as if I had shot a gun. The three kids on Riley dropped to the ground. Joey gave his little buddy one final whack with the nerf bat.

"Listen up," I said. "Where's Ben?"

"Here."

Samantha and I looked around, but we couldn't spot where the voice had come from.

"Where?"

"Here!" He crawled out from behind the couch. Dust balls clung to his hair and his clothes. "I was looking for a marble."

Samantha grabbed my hand with her cool fingers. She let out a deep breath. I hadn't realized how scared she was until then. She let go of my hand, probably not even knowing she'd grabbed it. I knew, though.

The little monsters began to bounce around the room again, screaming and yelling. I began to feel like the "before" part of a headache commercial.

"This is nuts," I muttered. I doubt anyone heard me. Not even Samantha, who was still close beside me.

I put my fingers to my mouth and whistled again.

It froze them all again. Except for Joey, who continued to hammer his friend with the nerf bat. I walked over and yanked it from him. He glared at me, but didn't say a thing.

"Listen up," I barked. I waved the bat in a general circle. "You are going to learn to do something with your energy. And it won't have anything to do with this chaos."

"Oh yeah?" some kid asked.

At the back of the room, another volunteer wheeled in a cart with a giant Kool-Aid container and plates of cookies. I knew I wouldn't have the attention of these kids much longer.

"Yeah," I said. "You guys know Riley Judd is the best hockey player in the WHL?"

"Maybe," the same kid said.

"You'd better believe it," I said, pointing the end of the baseball bat at the kid and looking him right in the eyes. "So you should consider yourselves pretty lucky."

"Um, why?" the kid asked in a quieter voice.

"Because he's going to teach you to play roller hockey."

The kids erupted in big cheers.

Samantha, standing beside me, leaned over to make sure no one overheard her. "Don't make promises you can't keep, Tyler Watson. You don't know how good you have it compared to some of these kids. I don't want to see you hurting them."

Riley pushed his way through them and put his face right up to mine.

"No way in the world I'm going to teach them anything," he said. "You've lost your mind."

"Got any better ideas for passing time around here?"

He frowned.

The kids continued cheering. This *was* a big deal to them.

"Besides," I said. "Do you really have the heart to tell them you won't?"

"I'll get you for this," he said.

"You already did," I told him. "Remember? I've still got one game left in my suspension."

Eight

He shoots! He scores!" Riley yelled, a big grin on his face.

Except this was one of the few times Riley himself wasn't scoring. Instead, it was Joey, the little kid who loved to whack his friends with a nerf bat. Joey had just hit a wobbly slap shot three inches high. The only reason he had scored was because the goalie—an eight-year-old—had thick glasses and could hardly see.

The audience to this street hockey game consisted of two people—Riley and me. We were both in sneakers and Winter Hawks sweats, standing at the side of a paved courtyard in the shadow of the church building, watching the kids bump a ball around with cut-down hockey sticks.

Joey ran up to us and grinned back at Riley, then licked his upper lip because his nose was runny.

"Great goal," Riley said. "I sincerely mean it."

"Don't lick that stuff," I told Joey. "Wipe it with

your sleeve. Real hockey players always wipe with their sleeves."

"No they don't," Riley said. "They do this."

Riley pinched one nostril shut by pressing a finger against it. Then he pointed his face away from us and blew an explosive snort to spray his other nostril clear. "See?"

"Cool," Joey said. He grinned again and nodded, then ran back to join the others in the street hockey game.

"Good example, Riley," I said. We had a gym bag filled with water bottles and towels near our feet. I reached down, grabbed a bottle, and squirted some water into my mouth.

He leaned on his hockey stick. "Someone's got to teach these poor kids some manners."

"If I didn't know better," I said, "I'd think you almost cared."

"Don't tell anyone," he replied, "but I do. These kids can grow on you."

I nodded in agreement as the two of us kept our eyes on the kids.

It was now late September. In the last two weeks, Riley Judd had firmly established himself as the league's top scorer. No surprise, I had firmly established myself as the team's fourth-line right winger. For the third year in a row.

And in these two weeks, Riley and I had firmly established ourselves as heroes among these kids—even though I'd made a mistake by promising them roller hockey without first realizing how much it would cost to get them all into in-line skates. So we had told them it would be safer to first learn the basics of stickhandling by playing street hockey in sneakers.

Fortunately they were just as happy with a bunch of old hockey sticks and the rules of street hockey, which we made simple for them. Rule one—hit the ball, not someone else. Rule two—try to knock the ball between the big rocks we set up as goal posts at each end of the courtyard. Rule three—no other rules.

What I found sad was how little it had taken to become heroes to these kids. They had such terrible family lives away from Youth Works that these street hockey games became the highlight of their week.

"What do you say, Tyler?" Riley asked, interrupting my thoughts. "Should we show these kids how the pros play?"

"Yup." I dropped the water bottle back into the gym bag.

Among cheers from the kids, Riley jogged to one end of the courtyard, and I jogged to the other end. I realized something else had happened in the last two weeks. Riley and I had drifted into a friendship. He was still a showboat, and I was still invisible, but when it was just the two of us—like here or driving in my Jeep— the differences didn't seem as great. If you ignored Riley's cockiness, he was almost likable.

"Okay, boys," Riley shouted as he got the ball, "pour it on!"

A gang of kids moved on him like ants on honey. We not only had the eight- and nine-year-olds, but also a good group of twelve- and thirteen-year-olds today. Our task wouldn't be easy.

Riley's arms and legs flashed as he danced around, slapping the ball back and forth with his stick. Somehow —and I doubt a slow motion replay could have showed how—Riley made it through the maze of players with the ball. He shouted and screamed as their sticks hit his shins, but he made it through. He kept the ball for five minutes, running in circles as the kids on both teams chased him and yipped in glee.

Finally, Riley stopped running in circles and headed toward where I guarded the goal at the open end of the courtyard.

I got ready to stop him.

Riley stopped, grinned, and flipped me the ball.

"I'm tired. Your turn."

"Thanks," I said.

The horde of kids moved on me.

I don't have the stickhandling skills that Riley does.

I decided instead to rely on keeping my distance from them.

Instead of heading toward Riley's net, I backed up, keeping the ball with me.

The paved courtyard was U-shaped. At Riley's end were some church offices. On both sides, two-story walls. On my side, the opening led into an empty parking lot.

They were coming at me like a pack of insane wolves.

I turned and bolted toward the empty parking lot, keeping the ball in front of me.

"Hey!" a couple of kids shouted.

"Get him!" a couple more shouted.

They all screamed and began to chase me.

This was fun.

I outran them easily, building my lead to at least twenty-five steps. When I reached the far end of the parking lot, I turned and faced them.

They were a wave of street warriors, yelling and grinning and waving their sticks, ready to pounce.

I waited until they were almost on me. Then I flipped the ball over their heads and ran around them, chasing down the ball toward my own net and the courtyard.

"Breeaaakkkaaawaayyyyy!" I yelled. And it was a breakaway. Longer than any breakaway in the history of hockey. The kids had turned to stampede after me, but they were well behind me. I had the empty parking lot ahead, all of the courtyard, and finally, far, far away, there was Riley at the other net, leaning on his stick and waiting for me to arrive.

I thundered toward him. I didn't need any fancy stickwork at this point. We used a street hockey ball—made of orange plastic and heavier than a hockey puck. It wasn't going to get stuck in the cracks of the pavement.

When I reached my own net again—with all of the courtyard ahead of me and the kids now thirty steps behind—I yelled, "Riley, prepare for the shot of doom!"

"Tyler," he yelled back, "you don't have a chance!"

I kept sprinting toward him. Then, without warning, I stopped. Close enough to have a good chance at scoring. Far enough away so that Riley would still have time to make the save if he was fast enough.

I set the ball up carefully and backed up two steps.

Riley knew exactly what I was going to do. He set himself up like a goaltender.

The kids were yelling and screaming.

"Ready, Riley?"

"Sure, marshmallow man!" he said, insulting my slap shot even before I hit it.

"Marshmallow?" I roared back.

The kids were almost on me. I couldn't wait any longer.

I raised my stick above my head, took the two steps, and timed it perfectly so that I was bringing the stick down and launching my body weight into the world's biggest, baddest slap shot.

I crunched that ball with everything I had.

And I watched it soar over Riley's head to smash directly through a window behind him.

 *Nine*

Oops," I said. I waited for someone to yell through the window at me.

Nothing.

The kids gathered around me.

"Well," I said, reminding myself I was supposed to be a good example, "I'd better go tell someone what I did."

"Hey, Tyler," little Joey said at the back of the crowd.

"Yeah?"

"When you're in there, if it looks like you're going to be in big trouble, can you at least throw us the ball?"

"Huh?"

"This street hockey is fun," he explained. "We want to keep playing."

"Thanks for the support," I said.

He nodded. I guess kids at that age have a tough time understanding sarcasm.

I waved at Riley. "See you in a few minutes."

"Tell you what," he said, "let them know we'll both pay for the window."

"It was my shot," I said.

He shrugged. "Our game."

I grinned. Riley was getting more human all the time.

I waved again and trotted toward the side doors that would let me inside the church building.

It wasn't difficult to find the office with the broken window. All I did was walk down the hallway and open doors until I found a room with natural air conditioning.

Finding the ball, however, wasn't so easy. There was no one inside the office to tell me where it went.

I saw gray steel filing cabinets against one wall. I saw a big gray steel desk in the corner of the other two walls. I saw a crooked chair on swivel wheels. I saw broken glass sprayed on the yellow tile floor. But I didn't see an orange hockey ball.

I dropped to my knees.

Naturally, the ball had rolled beneath the desk, right into the far corner.

I looked around for something to use to reach the ball. Nothing.

I'd have to get on my hands and knees and crawl.

I pushed the chair away and crawled into the opening beneath the center of the desk. I bent lower and reached into the corner. My fingertips just barely touched the ball. I stretched farther.

Then I heard footsteps in the hallway, coming in

my direction. And I heard voices. I recognized one voice as Samantha's.

How good would this look, me with my hind end pointing at the ceiling?

I grunted and stretched as far as I could, finally able to get enough of the ball to roll it toward me. I grabbed the ball and backed out.

My sleeve snagged on a screw that poked out of the bottom of the desk.

The voices grew louder.

For a moment, I nearly yanked hard. But it felt like I was stuck good, and I didn't want to rip my Winter Hawks sweat jacket.

The voices moved past the open door and continued down the hallway. Two voices. Two sets of footsteps. The other voice belonged to a man. I didn't recognize his voice.

There was a click as the door to the office next to me opened.

"Step inside, Samantha," I heard the man's voice say. The clearness of the sound surprised me. Then I saw the vent on the wall, just inches from my face. I easily guessed that's how I was able to hear.

I was still stuck, though. I tried wiggling my arm. It didn't help.

"I don't understand what this is about," Samantha told him.

I didn't want to listen. Their conversation was none of my business. I made myself into a pretzel and tried to reach my sleeve with my other arm.

"Sit down," the voice said. "It's about your brother."

I heard her gasp. "He's all right, isn't he?"

"Yes," the man's voice said, "for now."

I frowned. His voice did not sound pleasant.

"You're still asking around about the kids," the voice said. "Didn't you get the note telling you to stop?"

"But—"

"But nothing. It wasn't an accident that your brother was taken. It was a warning. Even if the muscle-brained jerk with the hockey stick hadn't gotten in the way, your brother would have been returned the next day."

"Tyler? He's not a—"

"Listen to me, Samantha. Listen good. You stop asking questions. Otherwise next time something permanent will happen to your brother. You could go to the newspapers. You could go to the police. You could let the whole world know about this. But your brother would be dead. Understand?"

I'd stopped caring about my sleeve.

There was long silence in the other office.

Finally Samantha answered the man. "I understand," she said.

"That's a smart girl."

There was a scraping of chairs.

He must have stood. Which meant they were leaving. Which also meant they might see me as they left the office.

I pushed hard, trying to get the rest of me under the desk.

Neither of them spoke as they left the office next

door. One set of footsteps headed one way. Another set headed the other. No footsteps stopped at this office and looked in to find me under the desk.

To get free, I had to slide and bend and work myself loose from my jacket. I backed out, then crawled in from another angle to unhook the sleeve from the screw. Then I tossed the ball down to the courtyard.

The waiting kids cheered.

Cheering or not, I didn't feel better.

On my way outside, I passed the office where Samantha and the man had been talking.

It didn't help my mood.

The sign on the door showed that the office belonged to Earl Chadley, director of Youth Works.

Ten

An hour later, when we got into the Jeep, Riley reached into the gym bag. He tossed the water bottle into my lap.

"Kool-Aid," he said.

I started the Jeep and began to drive.

I didn't start drinking.

"Aren't you thirsty? We ran those kids ragged. I hope we'll have energy for practice."

"Yeah," I said. It was six o'clock. We had a half hour to get to the rink and another half hour to get dressed in hockey equipment. It was going to be a light practice tonight, since tomorrow was a game day.

Riley guzzled from his own water bottle. He smacked his lips. "Good stuff," he said. "I borrowed it from their snack cart. You know, the one with the cookies and big Kool-Aid jugs that shows up for the kids."

"Yeah," I said.

"I guess you can't really say we're borrowing this

Kool-Aid," Riley said. "I mean, they probably wouldn't want it back when we're through with it. Or when it gets through us."

"Yeah," I said, finally drinking some Kool-Aid from my own water bottle.

"What's the matter?" Riley asked. "I just made a joke."

I drank in silence.

"Did Samantha turn you down?" he continued. There was a high school dance coming up. I'd made the mistake yesterday of mentioning to Riley that I'd like to take Sam to it.

"Didn't ask her," I said. At least I hadn't asked her about the dance. After tracking her down, I'd told her about the window. Then I had worked up enough courage to ask her why her brother was in danger. She'd gotten angry and told me to mind my own business.

"You've got to go for it," Riley said. "Only two weeks until the dance."

I turned a corner and headed past the Chinatown gate toward the Burnside Bridge.

"She might say no," I said. My mind, though, was on Earl Chadley, director of Youth Works. Riley and I had met him only briefly. He had introduced himself to us on our second visit and thanked us for our help with a big smile that didn't seem real.

Earl Chadley was a skinny man with long hair that he flipped back while he was speaking. He wore sandals and blue jeans and a ratty old shirt, which might have been cool if he were twenty instead of closer to fifty.

Why was he threatening Samantha Blair with something as serious as killing her brother? What secret did she know that she was supposed to keep hidden? What were the questions she wasn't supposed to ask?

"Hey, Watson, snap out of it," Riley said, "I was telling you something."

"Sure," I said. "What?"

"It's advice," Riley said. "The only way you get anywhere in life is by taking chances."

"Sure," I said.

He snapped his fingers. "It's the window, right? You're bummed out about that. I already told you, I'll pay for half the damage."

"Don't worry about it," I said. My mind was still on Samantha and the weird conversation I had overheard. "There are a lot worse things in life than broken windows."

I found myself yawning as we skated our warm-up patterns to begin the practice.

I moved past a bunch of guys leaning and stretching from side to side to loosen up. I put on a burst of speed and caught up to Riley.

"I think it was a dumb idea to play street hockey before practice," I said, cruising beside him. "My legs feel like wooden stilts."

Riley didn't answer.

"Hey! Goofball. Didn't you hear me?"

He turned his face toward me. He had a strange frown. It crunched his face into a look of worry.

"You all right?" I asked.

He stumbled, then caught his balance. "I don't know." He stumbled again.

Now panic crossed his face.

"Tyler!" I heard fear in his voice.

Someone fired a pass in our direction. The puck bounced off his skates.

"Tyler!"

"I'm right beside you," I said. The fear in his voice scared me too.

"Skate closer," he said. "Let me grab your arm."

I moved tight beside him. With his hockey glove still on, he pulled at my sweater.

"Get me to the players' bench," he said. "Move slow, so it looks like we're talking about stuff."

"I don't get it," I said.

"Just do it, all right?"

Guys skated past us. Some were moving at full speed, getting ready for the regular skating drills that Coach Estleman used to keep us in shape.

I felt like a boy scout helping an old lady across the street.

"We there yet?" he asked.

"Don't be dumb," I said. "You can look for yourself."

"No," he said. "I can't."

"Huh?"

"Tyler," he said. "I have weird allergies. Sometimes they act up. But never this bad."

He stumbled a bit.

"I'm scared," he said, "real scared. I can't see. It's like the whole world is gray."

Eleven

It took Riley an hour to get his vision back. Although he could see again, he was no longer the same person he'd been before. I discovered that a few days later as we were driving toward Youth Works for our next visit. Riley turned down the volume of the car stereo.

"Why you listen to country music is beyond me," he said.

I took my right hand off the steering wheel and turned the volume up again. "Because I can understand the words."

I braked hard to miss a truck that had suddenly slowed in the left lane.

He took advantage of the distraction and turned the volume down again. "Words? That's dumb. It's called *listening to music*, remember? You jam a CD in your stereo and listen to *music*. Not *words*."

Safely past the truck, I turned onto Fifth Avenue, toward Youth Works. I also turned up the volume. Again.

"It's not music when the singers are screeching like they've slammed their fingers in a door."

He turned the knob down. Again. "Sometimes you act like an old man," he said. "'Screeching singers' is something my dad would say."

I turned it up. "I act like an old man?"

He turned it down. "Yeah, an old man. Like you don't want to take chances."

I turned it up. "If I need a psychologist, you'll be the first person I call."

He turned the volume down.

"Riley . . ." It wasn't funny anymore.

"Could be I'm the one who needs a psychologist," he said. His voice was quiet and serious. "Do you think about God? About dying?"

I left the volume turned down. Maybe I hadn't heard him right. "Dying?"

"Dying," he repeated.

I let the word hang in the air, trying to decide what to say. I believed in God. But I didn't know what to say to Riley. So I just listened.

"Look," he said, "I trust you. But if you ever tell any of the guys on the team I started talking about this, I'll kill you."

"I won't say anything. But why are you thinking about—"

"Dying?"

"Yeah," I said. "I mean, we're hockey players. We're not supposed to think."

"We're also not supposed to suddenly go blind for an hour for no reason at all."

"I agree," I said. "That was weird."

It had been weird. Although a couple of days had passed, the doctors were still no closer to figuring out what had happened to Riley during practice.

"Tyler, I'll admit I was scared when everything went gray. You know that."

For the next few seconds we both thought about his losing his sight as I slowed the Jeep in front of the Youth Works building. I pulled on the parking brake and half opened my door.

Riley's voice stopped me.

"Nothing like that ever happened to me before," Riley said. "I've never felt helpless like that. I was blind for an hour, but I didn't know if my vision would ever come back. Now, I keep wondering if I'll suddenly go blind again. And what if I stay blind?"

"Well, you could always get a job as a referee."

"This is not the time to be funny," he said.

I snapped my mouth shut.

"So I started thinking about my heart," Riley continued. "I mean, there it is, pumping blood all by itself without me telling it to. What if it stopped all of a sudden, for no reason—just like I went blind for no reason. For that matter, why *does* my heart keep beating? Every night since then, I haven't been able to fall asleep because when I think about my heart stopping, I think about dying and what happens after that."

The Jeep door was still half open. I closed it. "Don't get me wrong," I said. "But is that why you've played the last two games so badly?"

Riley had managed only one assist in two games.

Both games had been against the visiting Lethbridge Hurricanes. We'd won 8–2 and 10–4, and Riley had only scored one point out of the combined 18 goals. Even the newspaper articles had begun to question his slump.

"My confidence is gone," he said. "Can you blame me? If my eyes can go, anything else can go. I half expect to go blind during a shift. Or keel over from a heart attack as I rush up the ice."

"It was a freak thing," I said. "Like getting hit by lightning."

He snorted. "Let me ask you this. If you got hit by lighting once and survived, wouldn't you be nervous to be outside in a thunderstorm again?"

I was beginning to understand his fear.

"You didn't get any warning about losing your sight, did you?"

"No," he said. "And I'd give almost anything to know why it happened."

"Listen up, guys," I shouted to get the kids' attention. "Weather looks good out there today. Anyone want to play some street hockey?"

As expected, they cheered. I didn't blame them. The Youth Works playroom was small and crowded. Normal kids would go crazy in here. And as Riley and I had learned during our visits here, this bunch was definitely so hyperactive they were beyond normal.

"Riley's got the sticks," I shouted. "Let's not tear down

the hallways as we go outside. Zip your lips and line up in single file."

I couldn't believe what happened next.

The kids stopped shouting and laughing and screaming and began to line up in single file.

Riley gave me a surprised look.

"They must like hockey," I said.

I stayed at the door, and Riley led them out.

I watched Ben, Samantha's brother. He was in the middle of the line. When he passed me, I patted his shoulder.

"How you doing?" I said. What I really wanted to ask him was if anyone had tried to kidnap him for the second time. I really wanted to ask him if he knew why the director of Youth Works was threatening his sister.

"I'm doing good," he said. "Can I be a goalie today?"

"Sure," I said. "Hey, what's with the cotton ball?"

He was wearing a T-shirt, and the cotton ball was obvious, taped to the inside bend of his elbow. I'd had the same thing myself after donating blood to the Red Cross.

"Blood tests," he said, like it was no big deal. "We all get them. Samantha says I have to leave it on until after dinner."

"Oh."

He marched onward. I followed him out of the room and down the hallway. I kept my eyes open for Samantha. She was always running around and doing different things around the building. If I was lucky, I could run into her and find an excuse to ask her to the

61

dance. There was only a week left. I didn't have the courage to call her by telephone.

But I didn't see her.

Fifteen minutes later, I had bigger things to worry about.

Joey, my favorite little red-head monster kid, stopped in his tracks in the middle of the courtyard. He toppled to his side as one of the other kids fired him a pass.

His head made a horrible sound as it hit the pavement. His body began to flop around. I got there just as his face was turning blue. Riley arrived a half second later.

"Ambulance?" Riley asked.

"Yes, hurry!" I said. This was no time to ask any other questions or think about anything else.

Riley dashed toward the Youth Work offices.

I dropped to my knees and leaned over Joey. He was wheezing, like he couldn't breathe.

I whipped off my jacket and folded it as a pillow beneath his neck. I pinched his nostrils together with the thumb and forefinger of my right hand. I pulled his chin down with my other hand. His face was cold and clammy.

"You'll be all right, little buddy," I said with a lot more calm than I felt. "Let's just get you breathing right again."

I began to blow air into his lungs.

Twelve

Sunday afternoon, as the referee skated into the face-off* circle deep in our end, I looked at the score board. Seven to six. We were leading this home game against the Kamloops Blazers. Ten minutes, twenty-seven seconds left in the game. A full house of screaming fans.

The players had lined up, waiting for the puck to drop. I didn't feel my usual nervousness. In the second period, I had scored a goal. I had tipped in a slap shot from one of our defensemen at the point. By scoring that goal, I knew Coach Estleman couldn't say I didn't contribute to this game.

I turned my attention away from the score clock and back to the game.

The referee slapped the puck down between the sticks of the centers. They fought for the puck. Our center spun his body around, blocking the other center. Our center kicked the puck back with his skate, sending it to our defenseman who was waiting behind the net.

By then, I was already moving toward the boards. As winger, that was my position. If we lost the puck and it squirted up to their defenseman on the blue line, I was close enough to keep him from shooting at our goalie. If we kept the puck, I was in position to take a pass.

This time, our defenseman fired the puck along the boards.

It began to bounce, and I knew I would have trouble trapping it with my stick. I backed up against the boards and turned my skates to trap the puck.

Unfortunately, this gave their defenseman time to rush down the boards toward me. He reached me just as the puck did. He hit me with a full body check, and spun me around.

I should have thanked him. He slid off me and fell to his knees. I ended up facing their net. And the puck was straight ahead, waiting like a plum for me to pick off a branch.

I sprinted forward. The crowd's roar grew. They could see what I saw.

Two of us Winter Hawks forwards. Only one defenseman left to protect the net at the far end. We had a two-on-one* breakaway!

I flipped the pass over to Steve Harper, the other winger, who had cruised into the open ice at center. He busted ahead at an angle, drawing the defenseman over to the side. I was skating at full speed too.

Harper and I had at least a ten-step head start on the next closest Blazer.

Wind filled my face; the roar of the crowd shook my whole body.

I kept to the middle of the ice, and when Steve and I crossed their blue line, I began to slow down. Just a bit. That forced the defenseman into making a move. He had to go wide to stay with Steve, or slow down to stay with me. If he stayed with me, Steve could go in alone on the goalie. If he moved to Steve, I would be free for a wide-open pass.

The defenseman decided to gamble. He stayed with Steve as long as he could, and as Steve went to backhand me a pass, the defenseman dove, hoping to block it.

The puck slid beneath him. Onto my stick.

I was at the top of their faceoff circle. Just me and the goalie. And thousands of fans screaming for me to bury the puck in the net.

It was the big chance to be a hero, and I didn't want it. *What if I tripped? What if I missed the net? I'd be a bum.*

I faked my head and shoulders to the left, dragged the puck to the right, and went to fire a cannon of a wristshot. Except the puck hopped over my stick and rolled back into my skates.

Desperate to take a shot, I kicked it ahead. I took a feeble slap at the puck and managed to hit a slow looping shot that the goalie gloved easily.

Not only had I missed scoring, but I had also missed in the ugliest way possible. And in front of nearly every person in Portland who cared about hockey.

The ref blew the whistle to stop the play. I hung my head in the sudden silence of the disappointed crowd and got off the ice as soon as I could.

Coach Estleman didn't say a word as I reached the players' bench. He didn't have to. I had a good idea of what was going through his mind.

Thirteen

After the game, Coach Estleman took me aside in the hallway and spoke with me briefly. What he told me did not put me in a great mood. He wanted to meet with me on Wednesday. I doubted he wanted to move me up to the first or second line, even if Riley was still playing badly.

Unfortunately, when I left the coach I had to hide my sour mood because Joey and his mother were waiting for me in the lobby of the ice arena. I had told Joey I'd meet them after the game for burgers and milkshakes.

It had taken the team awhile to shower and to listen to the coach's post-game talk, so the lobby was nearly deserted. Joey and his mother saw me right away and walked in my direction. Joey looked fine, which was amazing considering that earlier in the week he had spent a night in the hospital hooked up to a breathing machine.

"Hey, Tyler," Joey said. He gave me a high five, which

I returned. I had visited him at the hospital, and when I found out they were releasing him, I had given him a pair of tickets to today's game.

His mother stood beside him. She was short, wearing an old jacket. Her hair was blond and stringy, her face pale and splotchy. I smelled cigarette smoke on her clothes.

"I'm Judith Scranton," she said. She bit her lower lip, "Joey's mother, but you probably guessed that."

"Hello," I told her. "I'm glad you were able to bring Joey to the game."

She shrugged. "You got us the tickets."

Her attitude threw me. Chances were good, the doctor had said, that I had saved her kid's life by giving him mouth-to-mouth. I'd given him hockey tickets. But it was like she didn't care. She looked every direction but in my eyes. She didn't smile. She fidgeted.

"Let's go," Joey said. "Tyler said we could get burgers and shakes."

"I told you," she hissed at him. "We can't afford it."

"My treat," I told them.

"No," she said. "You already done plenty. I'm not going to owe you more."

"But—"

"Nope. We may be poor, but we don't need charity from strangers."

"Mom . . ." Joey said. He was squirming.

"But Mrs. Scranton—"

"*Ms.*, if you don't mind. And if Joey and I don't hurry, we'll miss our bus."

Bus? This wasn't an easy place to reach by bus, not from the part of Portland where they lived. By giving them the tickets, I'd forced her to spend hours on a bus?

"I can give you a ride," I said.

She shook her head no. "We'll be fine."

"But—"

"We'll be fine," she said. It began to dawn on me that she was very uncomfortable around me. It also began to dawn on me that I felt uncomfortable around her.

Here I was, in nice new dress pants, polished dress shoes, a leather jacket, and with a haircut that might have cost more than the old coat she wore. Joey's dirty clothes were little more than rags, his fingernails and hair were grubby, and there were holes in his running shoes.

Was her life so tough that she didn't want to be reminded of another world, where teenaged kids had Jeeps to drive and she was forced to take the bus?

"It was nice meeting you," I finally said.

"You too," she said, her lips tight. I wondered how much begging Joey had done just to get her to the game.

"See you later, Joey," I said. "Down at Youth Works, right? Get ready for some big-time street hockey."

"No," Mrs. Scranton said. "You won't see him there."

"I beg your pardon?"

"You won't see him there." Her voice became angry. "First they pay me to get Joey in the program. And right when it seems things are finally right with him, they kick him out."

I looked at Joey. He nodded, with a miserable look on his face.

"Yeah," he said. "First Nathan and Drew and Jamie. Now me. It ain't fair."

"I don't get it," I said. "Nathan and Drew and Jamie. Who are they?"

"Kids," he said. "Youth Works kids. They got sent to the hospital too. Just like me."

"Just like you?"

He nodded gravely. "Yup. Seizures."

Mrs. Scranton glared at me like it was my fault Joey was out of Youth Works. She pulled Joey away and headed for the exit, leaving me to stare at them with an open mouth.

Four kids with seizures?

They were almost to the outer doors by the time I caught up to them.

"Mrs. Scranton," I said, "would you mind if Joey told me the last names of those other three kids?"

Fourteen

I marched into Sam's office. It was exactly a week since Joey had had his seizure.

"I'd like you to tell me what is going on," I said to her.

Without getting up from her desk, she looked at her watch. "Well, for the next two hours, you and Riley will be playing street hockey with the boys." She smiled. "I can't tell you how much it has meant to them. Thanks."

"You know that's not what I meant," I said. "I've been here often enough to know the Tuesday afternoon schedule."

She pushed her chair back and stood. The tone of my voice was telling her plenty.

"All right," she said. She spoke slowly, half curious, half concerned. "What do you mean?"

It was strange. Being angry had taken all of my shyness out of me. I was able to speak directly to her, without staring at the floor.

"What do I mean? For starters, Joey's not the first kid to have a seizure here."

"How do you know—"

"And he isn't the second kid to have a seizure here, either. Isn't he the fourth kid in four months to get sent to the hospital?"

"But—"

"Joey and his mother came to our game on Sunday afternoon. It was my first chance to speak to him since the hospital. He told me about three of his friends. Maybe you remember them. Nathan. Drew. Jamie. All of them had seizures. Right?"

"Yes, but—"

"And all of them have been told not to return to Youth Works. Any reason?"

She took a deep breath and blinked a couple of times. "Insurance," she said. "It's difficult for organizations like ours to get insurance against being sued. We can't afford the risk of keeping kids who have proven they are likely to have seizures."

"Interesting," I replied. "Very interesting. Almost as interesting as finding out all four of them have ADD. Do you think that's a coincidence?"

"ADD?" Samantha blinked a few times again. "I don't understand."

"Attention deficit disorder. You know, a medical condition that some kids have. It makes them hyperactive, and they can't pay attention to anything for long. I find it strange that someone in your position pretends not to know what it is."

She blinked more. "I'm not pretending."

But she *was* pretending. I'd already made some phone calls. I'd already visited the mothers of Nathan and Drew and Jamie. Because of that, I knew Samantha was lying.

Her constant blinking seemed odd. I wondered if I could guess what it meant.

"And you don't know why Ben was kidnapped?" I asked.

"He just happened to be in the wrong place at the wrong time," she said. "It's not like someone was looking for him specifically."

This time, I expected her to blink. Which she did.

"If you want to lie to people," I said, "you should learn to be a better actress. You give yourself away by blinking. You can't look me in the eyes when you lie."

"You are rude. Please leave."

"I might be rude. But I do know Ben is in danger. In fact, I know you're supposed to keep your mouth shut about something or he'll get seriously hurt."

Her mouth dropped. "You can't know that," she managed to say in a whisper.

"I overheard Earl Chadley threathen you. I know plenty more too. After Joey told me about Nathan and Drew and Jamie, I called each of their mothers. Not only did I find out that all of the boys have been diagnosed with ADD, but I also found out every one in our group suffers from it. Almost like you went out and collected kids who have ADD."

That, of course, explained why they were so crazy

and wild during our visits here. If it hadn't been for the street hockey to tire them out, Riley and I would have gone equally crazy trying to work with them.

"I found out something else," I said. "Joey, Jamie, Nathan, and Drew had been making great progress. Every one of their mothers was sad to see them out of the program because every one of their mothers said the boys were so much quieter at home after time at Youth Works."

I took a breath. "What I don't know is the big secret you're hiding. And I want to know it. Now."

"Drop it, Tyler," she said. Her face was white now. She wasn't blinking. "Drop the questions. Drop your volunteer time here. Drop everything and pretend you never once called those mothers. Then go back to hockey and forget you ever heard of Youth Works."

"Why?" I said. "Give me one good reason why."

"Because you look much nicer in a hockey uniform than you would in a coffin."

Fifteen

Mr. Cranky Pants," Riley said to me as we walked away from the Youth Works building toward my Jeep. "What's the matter? Did Sam turn you down for the dance?"

Two hours had passed since my conversation with Samantha. Riley and I were both dripping sweat after a long run with the kids. I carried my gym bag in one hand, my Jeep keys in the other.

"I didn't ask her," I said.

"You spent enough time in her office when we got here," he said. "How could you not have asked her?"

Riley carried his own gym bag over his shoulders.

"You want to hear something crazy?" I asked.

We were almost at the Jeep.

"Sure."

I waited until we were both inside. Riley threw his gym bag on the floor at his feet. I put the key in the ignition. We both pulled our seat belts on.

I didn't start driving, though. Instead, I told Riley about the weird things I had discovered with my phone calls. An entire group of kids with ADD. Four kids with seizures in four months. The mothers unhappy that the kids weren't allowed to come back to Youth Works.

"Well no kidding," Riley said with his usual smart-aleck grin. "Sometimes ADD kids use medication. So if your kid came home happy and tired and quiet, wouldn't you want him to stay in the program?"

Program.

That word kept going through my mind as Riley dug through the gym bag for his water bottle. He found it and offered it to me.

"Kool-Aid?" he asked. "I took some more from their snack tray while they weren't looking."

"Sure," I said. I gulped down some Kool-Aid and handed it back to him.

Program. Drugs.

I remembered the kidnapping van. It had been stolen from a pharmaceutical company. I remembered how it bugged me that the van had clean sides but a dirty back end.

Program. Drugs. Pharmaceutical company. What could it mean?

Riley almost had the water bottle to his mouth when I grabbed it from his hands.

"Hey! I'm willing to share! You don't have to be a jerk about it."

"Riley," I said. "You're allergic to a lot of things, right?"

"So?"

"I'm not. Which means I can handle a lot of things that you can't."

"So? What's your point? I'm thirsty. I'm not allergic to Kool-Aid, and I'm the one who got it for us. I deserve a drink as much as you do."

"No problem," I said. "Just answer me a couple of questions. When was the last time you had some of their Kool-Aid?"

He thought about it for a second. "Not the last time here. Joey had a seizure and I didn't get a chance to fill the bottle. So it was the time before."

"Exactly."

He nodded.

"Here's my other question," I continued. "When was the practice where you went blind for an hour?"

It took him much less time to answer this question. "Last time I had their Kool-Aid."

I remembered how my legs felt like wooden sticks. I hadn't gone blind like him, but I hadn't been my normal self either.

His eyes dropped to the water bottle in my hands. He repeated himself. "Kool-Aid! Are you trying to tell me . . ."

I offered him the water bottle. "Still want to share?"

He shook his head no.

"The Kool-Aid," I said. "And I wonder if that also answers a lot of other things."

Sixteen

When I settled into the corner chair of Coach Estleman's office on Wednesday afternoon, he didn't waste any time getting to the point.

"Tyler," he said, "on Sunday afternoon, with ten minutes left in the game, you had a chance to score the goal to put away the Blazers. Remember?"

I nodded yes. I did remember. It would have almost been better if I hadn't even had the chance in the first place.

"And you couldn't have made it easier on the goalie if you had picked up the puck and handed it to him. Remember?"

I nodded yes again. I was highly aware of my gym bag at my feet. Whatever might happen during the next ten minutes of discussion, I had a question of my own.

"I know why," he said. "I know exactly why you didn't bury the puck. You had already scored a goal. You thought one was enough."

"Well . . ." I said. He was probably close to the truth, but I didn't want to admit it.

"Tyler," he added, "you cause me as much grief as any player I have ever coached."

I thought back over the three years I had been on the Winter Hawks with him as my coach. I hadn't once missed curfew. I hadn't once yelled at him. In fact, I hadn't even been late for a single practice.

I mentioned all of this as I defended myself.

"I almost wish you would give me that kind of grief," Coach said. "At least I'd know what to do about it. I could bench you. Or I could fine you. But what's it going to take to get you to play good hockey?"

His face showed concern. I think that made it worse. He wasn't mad. He wasn't disappointed. He was, if anything, sad to be needing to talk to me.

"You see," he went on, "you're big enough, you're talented enough. You can shoot." He winced, no doubt remembering how I had hit him below the belt buckle during one practice. "Yup, you can shoot. But only in practice, not games. Same with your skating and stick-handling."

He paused and stared at me. "So what stops you from playing good hockey in game situations? You're not afraid to go into the corners and dig the puck out. When people push you around, you don't back away. We've kept you on the team this long because we keep hoping some day you'll break through and play the way you can. I half think you're just happy to be wearing the team jacket. But you don't want to face any pressure."

I let out a deep breath. "You're going to cut me from the team, aren't you?"

He slammed his fist on his desk. He half stood. He yelled down on me. "Listen to your tone of voice! You don't even care!"

"That's not true," I said, "But—"

"Don't tell me you care! Look at you! Sitting there like we were discussing the weather. You're accepting whatever happens! Like if I cut you from the team after two years, it's no big deal!"

He pounded his fist again. "Where's your fire, Watson? What's it going to take to get you to do more than wear the team jacket?"

He repeated himself, spitting the words at me. "Where is your inner fire?"

Coach Estleman sat back down and found his breath. He stared at me until I looked away. When he spoke again, he had himself under control.

"Do you think it was an accident that I paired you with Riley Judd? Sure I wanted you to help make him a team player. I didn't lie about that. But I was also hoping some of his fire would rub off on you. I was hoping you'd get mad enough and jealous enough of someone like him to actually play the way I know you can."

He snorted. "Hmmph. It's more like you managed to tie him to the same piano you drag around on the ice during hockey games."

Coach Estleman got up and started pacing around the office. He spoke more to himself than to me. "I've got Riley Judd, a million-dollar player who's starting to play like a ten-dollar player. And I've got you, a ten-dollar player who doesn't know he can play like a million-dollar player. Maybe my mother was right; I should have gone into pro wrestling."

He continued to shake his head and grumble beneath his breath as he paced.

"I don't want to get cut," I said to his back.

He whirled and glared at me.

"What's that?"

"I don't want to get cut."

He moved directly in front of me, crossed his arms, and stared down at me.

"I can't quite hear you, Watson."

"I don't want to get cut." I kept my voice even.

"Louder. You sound like a ballerina."

"I don't want to get cut."

"Shout it!"

I stood and stared right back into his eyes. "I am not going to play your dumb army-sergeant game. I will not shout like this is some kind of pep rally. But I will tell you this again. I want to play."

He grinned. "Finally. I see some fire in your eyes. You've got two more weeks, Watson. Show that fire on the ice, and you'll stay on the team."

I did not grin in return. My teeth remained gritted.

"We have a light skate in forty-five minutes," he said. "You'd better get moving. And tonight, play hard."

I did not move.

He arched his eyebrows in surprise. "Yes, Tyler? Anything else?"

"Coach," I said. "It's about the piano you blamed me for tying to Riley Judd."

"This ought to be interesting," Coach Estleman said.

"You know how sometimes players are tested for drugs?"

His face grew dark. "Drugs? Is Riley Judd into drugs?"

"Nothing like that," I said quickly. "I'm just hoping you know which doctor to call for drug testing."

"What exactly do you want to test?" he asked. He was frowning.

"This," I said. I leaned forward and pulled a water bottle out of my gym bag. "It looks and tastes like Kool-Aid, but I think it's a little stronger than the regular stuff."

Seventeen

A cut requiring five stitches definitely hurts. But it didn't hurt near as much as the smirk on Coach Estleman's face.

"Yup, five stitches, Coach," Scotty, our trainer said again, "maybe six. That flying puck cut him good."

Less than a minute earlier, I had been standing in front of the Medicine Hat Tigers' net, hoping to deflect a puck in for a goal. Instead, when our defenseman had fired the slap shot from the point, the puck had ticked off the stick of a Tigers forward as he tried to block the puck. It had changed direction too quickly for me to duck and had nicked the edge of my jaw, sending me to the ice and stopping the play.

Now, I was sitting in the players' box. Scotty had my head tilted backward to examine the bottom of my jaw. All I saw above me was his face. Along with Coach Estleman's face and that know-it-all smirk.

I felt the warmth of blood as it trickled down my

throat. Scotty wiped it away with a towel. On the ice, play continued. The third period had just started, and we were ahead of the Tigers, 5–3.

"Pretty deep cut, Scotty," Coach agreed. Out came another smirk. "It's the perfect excuse for Tyler to leave the game. An injury sounds a lot better than just plain quitting."

"Unnunnh." I tried to say. It is difficult to speak when someone is holding your chin. I yanked my head away. More blood gushed down the skin of my throat. I pulled the towel out of Scotty's hand and pressed it against the cut.

"Butterfly it," I said. "The stitches can wait."

"You're sure?" Coach Estleman asked. "If you step back onto the ice, you're going to face pressure. Leave now, and you can walk around the stands with your Portland Winter Hawks jacket and look cool."

"Butterfly it. I want to play."

Coach's smirk changed to a grin. "This afternoon's talk made a difference?"

"I want to play."

Coach nodded at Scotty. "Butterfly it. The boy wants to play."

Coach Estleman left me and started his usual pacing behind the players. He shouted instructions to players jumping onto the ice as others stepped into the players' box. I could barely hear him above the crowd's constant noise.

Scotty opened the first-aid kit and took out a bottle of iodine and a butterfly-shaped bandage. He dabbed iodine carefully over the cut, then used the bandage to pull the skin together tight enough to stop the bleeding until the game ended. They would send me to the hospital for stitches later.

The good thing about getting cut in the heat of a game is that the pain doesn't hit until much later. I was ready to play. One shift later, Coach Estleman sent me onto the ice.

Fine, I told myself. *Coach thinks I'm a quitter? I'll score a goal and then make him eat the puck for breakfast.*

Although the crowd was roaring its usual hometown support, I didn't look around the stands the way I usually did. I only had eyes for the puck.

Our shift began with a faceoff on the left side in the Tigers' end. The ref dropped the puck. Pat Casey, my center, managed to pull the puck back toward our defenseman on the Tigers' blue line.

Casey broke hard for the net.

Instead of clogging the middle by breaking for the net myself, I drifted backward, finding open ice.

John Mason, on defense, faked a slap shot.

The Tigers' forward, rushing up, fell for the fake and dropped, sliding with his body stretched to block the shot. John easily pulled the puck to the side, and the Tigers' forward slid harmlessly by.

I yelled for the puck. I had my stick high in the air, ready for a slap shot.

John snapped a pass toward me. It was coming so fast, I didn't have time to think about what I was doing. I just reacted, going into motion the way I had done hundreds of time in practice.

Timing it perfectly, I hammered my stick down at full

speed just as the puck arrived. I redirected the puck, slapping it two feet off the ice at the net. It drove through a maze of players and found the mesh of the net behind the goalie.

The red light blinked as the goal judge behind the Plexiglas confirmed what I already knew.

I'd scored!

I was mad enough at Coach Estleman that I didn't raise my arms in triumph, the usual reaction any time a player scores. Instead, I shrugged like hitting the prettiest slap shot of my life was just routine.

I'd scored so quickly that our line still had plenty of time left on this shift.

In my head, everything seemed quiet, like I had no thoughts. No worries. Just a calm peace and total concentration on the puck. Almost like when Sam and I had chased the kidnappers and they'd stepped out of their van armed with switchblades. Then, I'd only worried about how I was going to protect myself. Now, I only worried about the swoosh of my skates on the ice, the click of the puck on my stick. I liked the feeling, the tightness of determination that seemed to fill my stomach.

Casey lost the draw at center ice. Their center drew the puck back to their left defenseman, directly ahead of me. I charged ahead.

As expected, the defenseman passed around me to the Tigers' center who was cutting through the middle. I turned back, and jumped into full speed, chasing down the Tigers' winger I was supposed to guard on my side of the ice. I followed the winger all the way to the top of our own faceoff circle, staying so close their center had no pass to my side and was forced to dump the puck behind our net.

John Mason, as defenseman, picked up the puck. I stayed along the boards, giving him an outlet if he needed to pass to me.

The Tigers' forward stayed right beside me, guarding against a pass to me, just like I'd earlier guarded against a pass to him.

In theory, I was playing my position. No one could fault me for staying along the boards and tying up my man. It was the safe play. Nobody could blame me for any mistakes if I remained there.

I pushed off the boards, catching the Tigers' forward by surprise.

All right, Estleman, I thought, *you won't be able to say I don't try.*

I busted for center ice, angling to keep myself open for a pass. I kept my stick down on the ice, giving the defenseman a target. I yelled for the puck.

He snapped it forward.

Out of the corner of my eye, I saw their defenseman. He'd moved up to body check me, hoping I'd have my head down as I tried to receive the long pass.

At the last second, I hit the brakes so hard that my skates skidded across the top of the ice. I braced for the hit, let the defenseman bounce off me, and then scrambled for the puck.

No thoughts cluttered my mind except to pump my

legs as hard as I could. I chipped the puck ahead, sprinted to go wide around the remaining defenseman.

He slashed his stick down across my arm, trying to knock the puck loose. I didn't feel any pain; I felt detached from anything but the single thought of getting the puck to the net.

Clear of the final defenseman, I cut back to the center of the ice. There wasn't much time left as I reached the net. Without thinking, I made a fake to the left, drew the puck back in near my skates, flipped it to my backhand side, pulled it out of reach of the goalie, and banged it into the net.

The crowd went berserk.

I didn't. I skated back to the bench as if scoring two goals in one shift was no big deal.

Coach Estleman thumped me on the back as I stepped into the players' bench.

"Great goals!" he shouted. "I knew you could do it!"

"Hmmph," I said.

I scored my third goal five minutes later, snapping a wristshot into the top left corner of the net from the top of the faceoff circle.

At the end of the game, two things happened.

Coach Estleman told me to expect to play on the second line next game. And he sent me to the hospital.

Scotty was right. The cut took five stitches.

Eighteen

Driving my Jeep, I was daydreaming about my hat trick* the night before. Because it was a Thursday afternoon, Riley was beside me on our way to Youth Works. We had hockey sticks for the kids in the far back portion of the Jeep, our gym bags in the backseat. We had made this trip twice a week so many times now that I didn't have to concentrate much to get us there.

As usual, just past the Chinatown gate, I swung into the right hand turn lane. One block ahead, the light was green. I signaled for the turn, and slowed down for the corner at Fifth Avenue. Although it was green for me, a pedestrian stepped onto the crosswalk in front of the Jeep, and I had to slam on my brakes.

That took me out of my daydream in a big hurry.

"What an idiot!" Riley said. "Honk your horn."

"No sense," I said. "I've already stopped."

At the front of our hood, the man turned to face us.

He had one hand in his pocket. There was something too familiar about his face.

Then I remembered! The walrus mustache!

He was one of the kidnappers who had taken Ben. He was one of the two men who had pulled a switchblade on me.

He grinned at the shock that must have shown on my face.

He stayed in front of the Jeep. Cars behind us began to honk.

I was too stunned to do anything. Besides, there was no place for me to go unless I ran him over.

He grinned more and motioned with his free arm like he wanted me to roll down my window. He pulled his other hand from his pocket and flashed us a switchblade.

"He's the guy!" I told Riley. "One of the kidnappers from the van!"

Riley didn't have a chance to reply. The rear passenger door clicked open.

We had been so busy staring at the guy in front of us that we hadn't noticed another man step off the sidewalk. Before I could react, the second man slid into the rear passenger seat, pushing the gym bags onto the floor.

"Boys," he said, "nice day isn't it?"

Riley spun around. "Get out of—"

"Shut your mouth, kid," the guy said with a sneer. "I've got a .45 Magnum pointing at your back. If I pull the trigger, it will blow the stuffing out of the seat and you'll be smeared all over the dashboard."

The other man walked around the side of the Jeep toward the rear door on my side.

"If you hit the gas, kid," the guy in the backseat said, "I pull the trigger on your friend."

The light was still green, that was how fast this had happened. Cars behind us kept honking for me to complete my right turn through the intersection. To them, it must have looked like I'd stopped to pick up a couple of friends. Despite the honking, I forced myself to wait until the second man got into the backseat directly behind me. He slammed the door shut.

He laughed.

"Thanks for stopping," he said. "Looks like a great day for a drive."

I was tempted to drop the Jeep into reverse and slam backward into the car behind me. A car accident would get these two out of the Jeep.

I lifted my hand to the gearshift.

"Don't try anything stupid," the guy behind me said. He spoke in a cheerful tone, as if we were old friends. "I'll slit your throat so deep your tongue will become a necktie."

I hesitated. The honking grew louder.

"And while people are trying to stop your bleeding, Ron and me will make another getaway. Understand?"

I eased the Jeep forward.

"That's better," he said. "You just keep taking directions, and you'll be just fine."

"This is nuts," Riley said. "You can't do this to us."

"We've got a switchblade and a gun," the second guy said. "I think we can do whatever we want."

Fifteen minutes later, we drove around the back of an abandoned one-story warehouse near the Willamette

River and stopped. They forced us out of the jeep at gun point and took us to the trunk of a huge, rusty, old baby-blue Cadillac.

The one named Ron banged on the top of the trunk.

"We're opening it up!" he shouted. "And we've still got the gun. Don't do anything stupid!"

Who was he talking to?

Ron fumbled with a set of keys and clicked open the lock of the trunk. The door swung upward, throwing dust in our faces. Coughing and a dirty face greeted us.

Samantha?

"Get in and make yourselves comfy," he told us. "The three of you can have a little tea party in there while we take you for a nice long drive."

"P. S.," he said with an evil grin. "If you start screaming for help, Louie here will fire a couple of rounds through the backseat into the trunk. And trust me, you won't have much room to dodge bullets."

Nineteen

Sam?" I asked in the darkness of the closed trunk. A tire jack pressed against my ribs. My elbows were folded below me. I was facing backward, between Samantha and Riley. Both of them were on their sides, almost curled against me. It was not my idea of a little tea party.

The Cadillac bounced over bumps in the warehouse parking lot. I couldn't see where we were going, but I could see where we had been. A tiny peephole had rusted through the trunk, giving me a small circular view of the world the Cadillac left behind.

"I'm okay," she said. "Just thirsty. The jerks grabbed me about three hours ago. Just as I was leaving my apartment."

"But why?" Riley said.

Sam didn't say anything to his question.

"The drug-testing program," I said. "Beckstead Pharmaceuticals."

"How did you know that?" Samantha gasped.

"Just guessing." Her brother had been kidnapped in a pharmaceuticals' van with a dirty license plate. Except the *sides* of the van had been shiny clean, as if someone had just thrown mud on the back to cover the plates—not like the van had driven through mud. So maybe the company had just *said* it was stolen.

"Ouch," Riley said as we hit a big bump. "Hey, Tyler, is that who put drugs in the Kool-Aid?"

"You guessed that too!" Samantha said with another gasp. "But how?"

I wished we were having this conversation in a police station. Or in Coach Estleman's office. Anywhere but in the locked trunk of a Cadillac with two lunatics taking us for a long drive.

"You know I overheard the director threaten you with Ben's safety. That started me wondering," I told Samantha. Actually, I told it to her feet, which were pressed into my shoulders.

"Am I right?" I asked.

She took so long to answer, I began to wonder if she had even heard me.

The Cadillac moved steadily through traffic. The peephole showed me plenty of cars behind us. An old lady in a Volkswagen Beetle. A family in a van. A business man in another Cadillac—much newer than this one—tapping his fingers impatiently on the steering wheel as he waited behind us for a light to change. All of these people in their own little worlds, and they had no idea there were three of us stuffed into the trunk of the

Cadillac right in front of them. It made me want to scream in frustration. But I didn't want to give the lunatics inside the Cadillac a reason to start firing bullets through the backseat into the trunk.

"Yes, you're right, Tyler," Samantha finally said. "But I'm not sure it does us much good at this point."

She explained. It took some doing, over the rumblings of exhaust pipes and through the stops and starts of the Cadillac as it moved through traffic. What she told us added to what I had already managed to guess.

The Youth Works kids were chosen to belong to the program if they came from single-mother homes and if they had been diagnosed with Attention Deficit Disorder.

Samantha said that most ADD kids were extremely bright. But because of various medical reasons, they tended to be hyperactive and had difficulty concentrating on one thing for any length of time. Sometimes, ADD kids take medication, and it helps them focus.

Single mothers with ADD kids were usually glad to have someone help them. Not only that, these mothers often received payment for letting their kids belong. They were told that the money was part of the Youth Works approach to helping kids in all areas of life. Youth Works wanted the kids to get better food and clothing at home. Because of the extra help and because of the money, the mothers didn't ask questions about the program. Especially since their kids came home calm after time in Youth Works.

The reason they were less hyperactive, of course, was the Kool-Aid. Or, rather, because of what was in the Kool-Aid.

The kids, as I had guessed, were part of an experimental program, run by a Portland company called Beckstead Pharmaceuticals. Although there was medication already available for ADD kids, Beckstead wanted to find faster-acting medication.

Samantha said that any pharmaceutical company that discovered a better way to treat ADD could make up to $50 million in profit in the first year alone.

New medications, however, have to be tested for years before the government approves them. Beckstead was in financial trouble and needed to get their new drug on the market much sooner. They didn't want to waste time having the government test drugs that might not work. Instead, they wanted to deliver something that would pass all tests as soon as possible.

That's where Youth Works came in. The kids came from backgrounds where parents would be unlikely to ask questions, where parents would not have the education or money to file lawsuits, even if they did suspect something was wrong. In fact, if a kid had a seizure, he wasn't allowed back to the program, just in case the parents started comparing stories and realizing how unusual it was for so many kids to have seizures.

They resulted from the experimental drugs in the Kool-Aid. Most of the kids were fine with it—Beckstead Pharmaceuticals did want a safe drug. But not everyone reacted the same way to the drug. Including Riley.

Because of his allergies, he'd gone blind for nearly an hour when all it had done to me was make me tired and stiff.

To run the experiments, the kids were watched and tested before and after their snack break. Some got Kool-Aid with the drug. Some got Kool-Aid without it. Those who did, however, usually calmed down. Riley and I had never noticed a huge difference in their behavior because we kept them running around playing street hockey.

Samantha, however, saw them every day in several settings and did see differences.

She also knew about the number of seizures.

She knew the kids all had ADD, except for Ben, who wasn't really part of the program.

She had seen the blood tests given to some of the kids and heard the excuses—that they were being tested for polio and other diseases that sometimes hit kids in poor neighborhoods.

She had begun to ask questions. But she had asked the wrong person, Earl Chadley, the director of Youth Works, not knowing he received tens of thousands of dollars in bribes to allow the ADD experiment to continue.

At that point, the two thugs in the front seat were brought in by Beckstead Pharmaceuticals. They had kidnapped Ben intending to scare Sam into silence before releasing Ben back to her.

Because of me, however, the kidnapping had failed. Sam had asked a few more questions, which had led to the conversation I had overheard the afternoon I broke a window with my slap shot.

Even so, nothing would have happened. Samantha was scared enough to keep her mouth shut, and the program might have continued.

Except for one thing. Me and my big mouth. Me and my big mouth the afternoon I had marched into her office and demanded that she explain some things.

"A voice-activated tape recorder?" Riley asked as Sam told us how they had discovered my interest in the Kool-Aid. "In your office, Sam?"

We had been in traffic for nearly twenty minutes. My body ached from bouncing around inside the trunk. My muscles felt cramped, my nose full of dirt. My skin was itchy too. I wondered if the trunk had bugs in it.

"That's what Ron and Louie, our two friends in the front seat, told me," Sam said. "A voice-activated tape recorder. When you think of all they have at stake, it shouldn't be a surprise. They needed to know everything that was going on around Youth Works. When Tyler barged into my office with all his questions, it didn't take them long to realize they needed to stop him too."

"But why me?" Riley asked. "I didn't ask any questions."

"You were at Youth Works with Tyler," she said. "They didn't know if you knew anything. And for all they had at stake, they weren't going to take any chances."

"They won't get away with this," I said. "I already gave some of the Kool-Aid to Coach Estleman. The tests will show something was in there. And Coach Estleman knows the Kool-Aid came from Youth Works."

"That's right!" Riley's muffled voice said. "Kidnapping us won't help keep this a secret! Once we explain that to Ron and Louie, they'll have to let us go. Otherwise, they'll be in even bigger trouble. I mean, it's one thing to throw a drug or two into some Kool-Aid. It's another to haul people away in a beat-up old car."

"Wrong," Samantha said.

The way she said it sent chills down my hunched back. She spoke as if she had no hope.

"Look," she said. "How do you think I know so much about all of this? Louie and Ron had a lot of fun telling me. They also told me about your Kool-Aid test. Do you think once they knew you were asking questions that they would take any chances at all?"

"Coach Estleman took the water bottle from my hand," I said stubbornly. "And he's not part of this. He *will* get it tested."

"Sure he will," she said. "But it won't be the Kool-Aid they used on the kids. Beckstead Pharmaceuticals has connections everywhere. And they've been watching everything you do. They knew the Kool-Aid was going to a lab to be tested. They switched the samples."

"Impossible!" I said.

"Impossible? Your team doctor is a man named Crozier, right?"

"Right," I said, suddenly feeling even worse, if that was possible.

"Just this afternoon Ron and Louie bragged about

how they had broken into Crozier's office and made it look like a robbery. Only their real reason was to switch Kool-Aid samples. When the tests come back, they will show nothing unusual."

"Great," I said. I kept looking out the peephole of the trunk. It might not do me any good to know where we were going, but I was doing my best to figure it out.

"It gets worse," she said.

"Worse?" Riley said. "I can hardly wait to hear this."

"Ron and Louie told me that Beckstead is ending the program. They're going to stop testing kids at Youth Works and look for another place to start testing kids. We came too close to finding the answers."

"You sure know a lot," I grumbled.

"That's the worst news of all," Samantha said. "They don't care what we know."

"Your point?" Riley asked.

"Did they hide their faces from you?" she asked him in return. "Are they worried you'll ever have a chance to testify against them in court?"

"No," he said. His voice was small. He knew what she meant.

"You see," Samantha said, "if they stop running the program at Youth Works and if there is no drugged Kool-Aid around to show it was used in an experiment, nobody can ever prove that testing was done."

"Nobody except for us," I said. I winced as the Cadillac bounced through a pothole.

"Exactly," she told us. "There was a reason they were happy to tell me everything. They know we won't have a chance to let anyone else know. I mean, there's a reason we're in such a junker."

I didn't dare ask.

"If the car was newer," Samantha continued, "it would cost them that much more when they drive it off a cliff into the ocean. Which is their way of making sure we keep our mouths shut forever."

Twenty

Well over an hour later we were still in the trunk. Through my peephole, I had watched the late afternoon light become dusk, then darkness. Since I had not been able to see the sun behind us, I knew we were driving toward the sun, which meant we were headed west, toward the ocean and a cliff. And a real long good-bye.

For most of that time, we had traveled on a highway, with the tires whining at high speeds on the pavement. There wasn't much traffic on this highway. As evening approached, I had seen only occasional headlights behind us.

The Cadillac began to slow down.

"This isn't good, is it?" Riley said. "We've got to do something before they reach the cliff."

I'd been thinking the same thing. *But what?* We couldn't kick the trunk open. If we tried, they would hear the noise, and they would be right there with the .45 Magnum and the switchblade. While I had been able to work my arms loose from under my body and I had fiddled with the trunk lock almost in front of my face, there seemed to be no way for me to open it. And again, they had the gun and switchblade.

Unfortunately, Riley was right. If the Cadillac was slowing down, it meant we were that much closer to the moment they would drive this car off a cliff.

I tried to remember what I knew about Oregon's geography. The Pacific Ocean was around eighty miles from Portland. If we had averaged 55 miles an hour since getting out of the city, it meant we were close. Too close.

The Cadillac stopped.

"Relax, guys," I said. "Traffic light. We're in some town." Through the peephole, I could see cars pulling up behind us. The cars were lit by street lights.

What town? I wondered.

I got my answer at the next traffic light. Although I couldn't see much through the peephole, by pressing my head as close as possible, I was able to read some signs. I saw a motel. The Tillamook Motel.

I passed the information on to Riley and Samantha.

"Tillamook?" Samantha said. "That's almost at the ocean. I remember some beach towns north of here."

"With high cliffs?" Riley asked.

"High enough," she said quietly.

Riley didn't say anything until the next traffic light. "Well, Tyler," he announced, trying to keep his voice cheerful, "at least I won't have to lie awake at night and worry if I'll go blind or if my heart will stop beating."

"And I won't have to worry about getting cut from the Winter Hawks," I said.

The Cadillac rumbled as it idled at the traffic light.

"Probably too late," Riley said, "but I just thought of something. When you die, it's one thing or the other."

"Do we have to talk about dying?" Samantha said. "I'm scared enough."

"Unless we find a way to pop the trunk open when this car hits the ocean . . ."

"Thanks, Riley," I said. "I was doing my best to ignore that."

"That's what I mean," he said. "I've always ignored the fact I would die. And that either God is really there, or he isn't. I'd never thought of that before. It's one or the other. And I guess I should spend some time thinking about it to at least make up my mind about what I believe before I die."

I kept my eye at the peephole. If this was the last I would see of the world, I was going to be as greedy as possible and see as much as I could.

"Are you talking about God because you're scared?" I asked.

"Of course I'm not scared," he said sarcastically, "I look forward to drowning in a Cadillac. Especially an old ugly one."

I saw a car a block away. At first, I didn't want to dare believe what I saw. When it passed beneath the next street light, I saw the light bubble on top. It *was* a state police car.

I nearly shouted the good news to Riley and Samantha.

Until I realized it wasn't good news. The troopers were right there, pulling up behind us, but there was no way we could get their attention.

I wanted to bang my head on the floor of the trunk. It would pop my stitches open, but who cared. This was like being on a raft in the middle of the ocean and watching search planes in the distance as they flew right by without seeing you.

The police car eased up closer. For a moment, I saw both officers' faces in the windshield. The driver was sipping from a coffee cup. The other had a half-eaten donut in his hand. Then the police car pulled up so close to the Cadillac's bumper that all I saw was the shiny silver grill.

"But a person might die any day, right?" Riley was saying. "Like if you stepped in front of a bus. Or a drunk driver hit you. Or . . ."

"Riley! Please!" Samantha said.

"I'm sorry," Riley said. "It's just that—"

"Enough already," she told him. "I thought jocks didn't think. You're supposed to be stupid."

I knew *I* felt stupid. There was a police car right behind us. I couldn't think of a single thing to do to get their attention. I wondered if yelling would get the attention of the cops.

Probably not. If they were talking with the windows closed, they wouldn't hear us. And Ron and Louie in the front would definitely hear.

On the other hand, if we were going to die anyway, what would we have to lose by shouting?

I lifted my head to get a good lungful of air, and my face tangled on some electrical wiring.

"All right then," Riley said. "I'll change the subject. How's this? Tyler wants to invite you to the high school dance, but he's too afraid. So I'll ask for him. Would you go with him?"

I kicked Riley. He grunted.

"Well—" Samantha said.

"Of course, you're going to say yes," I said. "We're about to die. You're not going to hurt my feelings by turning me down to a dance we'll never get to."

It made me mad that Riley had embarrassed me. I slapped at the stupid wires. I sucked some air in again and almost began to yell, even knowing how useless it would be.

Then I realized what the wires meant. Now I might be able to get the attention of the police in the car behind us.

I grabbed the wires and yanked as hard as I could.

Twenty-One

The Cadillac took off slowly when the traffic light turned green. One minute later—I was counting the seconds heartbeat by heartbeat—I saw the sweetest sight I'd ever seen.

Red and blue flashing lights filled the tiny circle of my peephole as the police car closed the gap and tried to pull us over. I told Riley and Samantha what was happening.

"Cops!" Riley said. "They're stopping this car?"

"I just hope Ron and Louie don't try to outrun them," I answered.

"But—"

I interrupted Riley. "Here's the deal. As soon as this car is stopped and the police get out of their car, start yelling and screaming and kicking the trunk lid."

"They'll shoot us if we make noise," Riley said. "Remember?"

"With the cops right there? Not a chance. Kidnapping is one thing. But are they going to murder us with the cops watching?"

We felt the Cadillac swerve as Ron and Louie decided to pull over. And why not? Ron and Louie probably didn't know about the rust hole that I was able to peek through. I was willing to bet they figured Riley and Samantha and I had no idea they were stopping for the troopers. If we didn't know it was troopers, we sure wouldn't be brave enough to make noise. If we didn't make noise, the troopers would have no reason to look in the trunk. So why risk everything by trying to out-run the police?

The Cadillac settled on its springs as it stopped.

I heard the crunching of tire on rocks as the police car stopped behind the Cadillac. Again, all I could see through the peephole was the shiny silver grill.

The police car doors opened and slammed shut.

Footsteps approached the Cadillac.

It was now or never.

"Guys," I said, "start pounding and screaming."

We did. We hollered and bellowed and kicked at the trunk lid. Dirt fell into my face and nostrils, and I choked as it coated the inside of my throat.

No bullets tore through the backseat at our noise. No screeching of tires as the Cadillac took off.

We found out later that as soon as the troopers heard the screaming and thumping, they pulled their guns and held them on the surprised Ron and Louie.

We kept hollering and screaming and kicking until the trunk popped open and a flashlight blinded us.

"Teenagers!" a deep voice said with great surprise. "Three of them."

He clicked the flashlight off. We were able to see his tall silhouette above us, the wide brim of his hat clearly outlined against the street lights.

"Come on out," he said. "You'll be fine now. Just tell us what this is all about."

We climbed into the glare of headlights and flashing lights. Louie and Ron were braced against the side of the Cadillac. The other policeman guarded them with his revolver.

"Tell you what this is about?" I repeated. I drew a deep breath. "Sir, I would be happy to do just that."

Within ten minutes, the state troopers had Ron and Louie handcuffed and in the backseat of the police cruiser.

The larger of the two troopers stood outside the cruiser, speaking into the hand-held mike of the police radio.

The shorter one joined me and Riley and Samantha.

"We've called for a back-up cruiser. The boys will take you to the station. We'll need to file a report. Don't be surprised if it takes a few hours. Are you okay with that?"

Riley and I gave each other high fives. I winced at the pain of my palms slapping on his.

"We're okay with that," Riley said.

The trooper pushed back the brim of his hat and surveyed us with his hands on his hips.

"Lucky for you that the tail lights on this old Cadillac burned out," he said. "Otherwise we would never have pulled it over."

"Um, I'm not sure it was luck," I said.

"What do you mean, son?"

I opened my hands and looked down at my palms. Both were cut where the wire had sliced through the skin when I yanked on the electrical wires.

"Well sir, last summer I was pretty mad at the police because I got a ticket when a fuse on my Jeep went out and my brake lights didn't work. But if I hadn't gotten that ticket, I would never have thought of the idea."

I showed him my hands. "I was hoping if I disconnected the wires to their tail lights, you would do the same to them."

The trooper laughed. "Impressive son, mighty impressive."

Another state police car arrived, ending our conversation.

Riley and Samantha and I walked over and climbed into the backseat of the second cruiser. I went first, then Samantha, then Riley.

The trooper in the front seat hadn't even taken the car out of park, when Samantha leaned her face close to my ear.

"Tyler Watson," she whispered. "The answer is yes."

"Pardon me?"

"The high school dance," she said. "The answer is yes. Unless Riley lied and got my hopes up for nothing."

"Friday night," I said quickly, before she could change her mind. "I'll pick you up at seven."

Twenty-Two

"How was the dance?" Riley asked as he saw me in the lobby of the ice arena. "Did you and Samantha smooch when you drove her home?"

"Very funny," I said. "Are you ready for the Seattle Thunderbirds?"

"Changing the subject are we?"

"She'll be in the stands tonight," I said. "Is that enough of an answer?"

"Sure." Riley grinned. He waved at a couple of the guys heading toward the dressing room for the usual pre-game warm-up.

"It's been a wild week, hasn't it?" he said, as we joined the guys.

"Yup." The cuts sliced into my palm were nearly healed. We had endured dozens of phone calls for newspaper interviews. We had faced police, lawyers, and television cameras. Most of it had happened because Ron and Louie had decided to testify against Beckstead

Pharmaceuticals in exchange for reduced jail sentences. Without their testimony to match ours, it would have been hard to prove that the ADD kids had been used in an experimental program. Now, because of upcoming lawsuits against the company, it looked like every one of the kids involved in the program would get a hundred thousand dollars, enough to help their families and put them through college when they were older.

Even Riley and I had gotten some reward money. Not much, just enough to buy in-line skates and hockey equipment for every kid in our Youth Works group. It sure had been fun watching them try out their new skates when we played street hockey with them.

Yes, it had been a wild week. But that was the past. This was now. I had a WHL hockey game to worry about. Coach Estleman had moved me to the second line, and I wanted to stay there.

"I've got a question for you," I said as we walked past Coach Estleman's office. He was sitting behind his desk. He gave us a friendly wave through the open door.

"Fire away," Riley said.

"Now that you're back to your usual one or two goals a game, what do you think of just before you score a goal?"

"Huh?"

"You've got the puck on your stick, a chance to score. What do you think of in that moment?"

Riley stared at me and scratched his head. "Nothing, I guess," he finally said.

"Nothing?" His answer didn't surprise me.

Riley frowned in thought. "It's like I'm in a zone. Just me and the puck and the net. I don't hear anything. I don't feel anything. So the answer is that I don't think about anything."

"Do you worry about missing the net?" I asked. "Falling down? Making a mistake? Becoming a hero? Winning the scoring race?"

"Not when the puck is on my stick."

I nodded agreement. "One more thing. Over the last few weeks you were worried about going blind. It took your concentration away, didn't it? That's why you hit the slump, right?"

"I'm not worried about going blind anymore, if that's what you mean. I haven't forgotten about the other stuff, like what happens when you die. I mean, if you think about it, you've got to wonder why people believe in Jesus, even though he died two thousand years ago." He grinned. "Heavy duty philosophy, eh?

I could learn from Riley. He never held back in hockey or anything else.

"Tell you what," I said, deciding that a person doesn't need to be invisible with what he believes. "Any time you want, let's talk about it."

"Not on the ice," he said, still grinning. "I'm through thinking and worrying out there. If you want the puck in the net, that's all you can have on your mind when the puck's on your stick."

"Thanks," I said. "You've said a lot I needed to hear." I gave him a grin and stepped into the familiar chatter and the familiar sweat and heat-liniment smell of the dressing room. I ducked a pair of socks someone was throwing at our goalie and found a place to sit.

As I dressed in my hockey equipment, I thought about what Riley had said. I also thought back to some of the other things that had happened in the last month or so.

I'd stepped out of the Jeep, armed with only a hockey stick against Ron and Louie with their switchblades. At the time, all I had been concentrating on was how to knock the knives from their hands. I hadn't worried about getting cut or about being a hero for Sam. My only thought had been on their switchblades and knocking them away.

When I'd fired a beauty of a slap shot into the corner boards and accidentally hit Coach Estleman, my only thought had been on ripping the puck. Not on where it might go. Not on whether it would score.

When I'd stepped into another slap shot and broken the window at Youth Works, again, my only thought had been on making contact with the ball. I'd been pure, fluid motion in perfect timing, with nothing in my head except the desire to smoke the shot.

The game against the Medicine Hat Tigers, I'd skated back onto the ice with a butterfly bandage on my jaw. I'd been so mad at Coach Estleman that all I wanted to do was skate hard and shoot hard. I hadn't worried about whether the shot missed the net, how the crowd would react, or if I'd be in the sports section of the newspaper the next day.

And in the trunk of the car, when I'd finally stopped

worrying about what would happen when we went off the cliff and had concentrated on getting the cops' attention, my mind had found a way to solve the problem.

All of this was interesting to me. Real interesting.

Part of what made Riley Judd so good in hockey was that he concentrated on the puck. Nothing in his head got in the way.

Could I learn to do the same?

I hoped so.

I slipped my shin pads into my hockey socks, taped the shin pads tight and snugged the top of my socks with my garters. I stepped into my hockey pants, and put my skates on, leaving them unlaced. I put on my shoulder pads and my elbow pads.

My helmet was on the bench beside me. Along with my Winter Hawks jersey.

All I needed to do was tie my skates, pull my belt tight on my hockey pants, get my sweater on, and strap my helmet into place.

I didn't, though.

I sat without moving for a couple more minutes, letting the chatter of the dressing room flow around me.

Maybe that was the key. I would concentrate on the task, not on the result. When I had the puck, I would try to get into the zone of nothingness where all that mattered was what I was doing in that very second.

Could I find that zone when I needed it?

Probably not every time. But I was willing to believe if I worked at it, I'd learn it better. And hockey would be more fun.

Someone slapped my shoulder. I broke out of my thoughts and looked up at Riley. He was already in his equipment, ready to step onto the ice for pre-game warm-up.

"What do ya say, Tyler?" he asked. "Gonna score a couple goals tonight with Samantha watching in the stands?"

"Tell you what, pal." I grabbed my sweater and pulled it over my head. "Don't be surprised when it happens."

Lightning on Ice Series

Rebel Glory

B. T. McPhee, the star defenseman of the Red Deer Rebels, likes his chances of making it as a pro. But he doesn't like the small "accidents" that may keep his team from making the playoffs—and keep him off the team. In the spotlight of high-pressure hockey, B. T. has no choice. Unless he can unravel the mystery, the team's season—and his own career—will surely end. (ISBN 0-8499-3637-3)

All-Star Pride

Hog Burnell is playing on a WHL All-Star Team touring Russia. The goal is to beat the Russian All-Stars in the best-of-seven series to be shown as a television special. Hog could use the money that will come with a series win by the WHL All-Stars. But it doesn't take Hog long to discover there's plenty more money to be made along the way . . . if he's willing to pay the price for it. (ISBN 0-8499-3638-1)

Thunderbird Spirit

Dakota Smith plays for the Seattle Thunderbirds. He's fast and smooth with a shot as deadly as most pros. Unfortunately, there are more than a few unwilling to accept a Native American in hockey. For Mike "Crazy" Keats, haunted by a troubled background that fast makes him friends with Dakota, it means hockey just got more complicated. Racial hatred takes Mike and Dakota into a web of violence and deceit that makes winning this year's championship the least of their concerns.
(ISBN 0-8499-3639-X; available 3/96)

Winter Hawk Star

Riley Judd is a star center for the Portland Winter Hawks. His great playing skills are exceeded only by his oversized ego, which gets in his way. Given the choice of working with street kids in roller hockey or getting kicked off the team, Judd takes what he thinks is the easy way out. Along with a teammate named Tyler Watson, he discovers that it could cost their lives to give the kids the help they really need.
(ISBN 0-8499-3640-3; available 3/96)

Western Hockey League

The Western Hockey League
Encourages You to Stay in School

The players of the Western Hockey League are working hard toward reaching the dream of playing in the National Hockey League.

That's not the only thing they are working hard at. They know that as hard as they work on the ice, it is important to work just as hard in the classroom. Education makes them better players and better people.

The Western Hockey League makes sure that all of its players have the opportunity to succeed all the way through high school and into college or university. Players work together with their teachers, counselors, and their teams to learn both on and off the ice.

WHL players know when the going gets tough, on or off the ice, you must never give up. A good education will help you make better decisions about what to do with the puck, or what to do in life situations.

Whenever you have a question or a problem in school, ask your teacher or your counselor for help. And no matter what, STAY IN SCHOOL.